By the same author

Kirk's Law
Ruben's Ruse
Robb's Stand
Hangman's Lot

Flint's Bounty

The town of Eagle Junction has two headaches. The firs
the prolonged drought and the second is the threat
revenge from the Galt gang. The town marshal, Al
Murphy, has killed Ben Galt, brother of the notorious Ja
Galt and on discovering the identity of the man he has kill
and anticipating Jack Galt's terrible revenge, Murphy fle
town. His deputy, every bit as alert to the danger, follows h
example.

Meanwhile, Dan Straker, a drought-stricken farmer, is
town loading up his last supplies from Arthur Flint's sto
Without supplies he's done for and Flint can no lon
extend credit to him. If only he had the money to dive
mountain stream . . . .

Then, a dangerous option is revealed to him. Will the
of money to solve all his problems be sufficient to ju
taking on a mission which will, in all probability, cost hir
life?

Flint's Bounty

BEN COADY

A Black Horse Western

ROBERT HALE · LONDON

ISBN 0 7090 7417 4

Robert Hale Limited
Clerkenwell House
Clerkenwell Green
London EC1R 0HT

Typeset by
Derek Doyle & Associates, Liverpool.
Printed and bound in Great Britain by
Antony Rowe Limited, Wiltshire

PROLOGUE

Captain Josh Lawson tosses feverishly. The sound of shot and shell pound in his head. The acrid smell of gunpowder clogs his nostrils. Men are screaming. Cannons are roaring. Rifles crack. Pistols flash. Blood and gore all round. From the smoke, the agonized cries of men dying. The light fades. Ghosts fill the twilight. The mud of the battlefield makes the grey and blue of Confederate and Yankee uniforms indistinguishable. Insane with fear, men shoot their comrades rather than gamble their own lives on waiting that vital second to make certain that the mud-caked, ragged man facing them is friend or foe. Lawson hears the snap of bone. His leg is on fire. Pain. Terrible pain. He shoves a man aside out of the line of fire of a Yankee rifle. He knows the man as Jack Galt. As Lawson falls, he draws his pistol and shoots the Yankee. The soldier, barely sixteen summers old, weeps. Josh Lawson cries with him and for him.

Someone is gently wiping away his tears.

'You're safe now,' a woman says, her voice soft and caring.

Josh Lawson's eyes open.

'You were having a nightmare,' the woman, dressed in the uniform of a Union nurse, tells him. The hazel eyes regard him compassionately. 'My name is Mary Duff,' she says.

CHAPTER ONE

'Hold it!'

The small gathering of mourners around the grave, mostly made up of town do-gooders who turned out to plant any stray who was shot in town, considering it their Christian duty, turned their heads Abie Murphy's way. The marshal, in quite a lather, pushed his way through the mourners.

'Open that damn coffin, Lucas!' he commanded the undertaker.

A shocked intake of breath rose from the do-gooders.

'Did you say—?'

Murphy impatiently shoved the stunned undertaker aside. 'I'll do it myself.'

'Really, Marshal,' the Reverend Clark protested. 'This is a Christian burial service, and as such—'

'What I've got do will only take a couple of seconds, Reverend,' Murphy interjected. 'Then you can spout them fine words from the Good Book all day long, if you want.'

The gathering fell back in shock as Abie Murphy began prising the coffin lid open with a hunting knife, the blade of which bent under the task. Addressing the undertaker, he growled, 'You nailed this *hombre* down real tight, Lucas.'

The hollow-cheeked undertaker retorted, 'A man's got a right to go well packaged into the next life, Marshal.'

'Not so well packaged,' Murphy grunted, as the lid began to give way, 'that God or the Devil would have to spend an eternity trying to get the bastard out of his box for saving or burning!'

Incensed, the Reverend Clark spluttered.

'Save it, Reverend,' Murphy barked, 'this is nearly over and done with.'

The coffin lid split in two. Murphy impatiently yanked the upper half of the lid off to expose the bloodless face of the corpse. An obscene, ragged black hole between the dead man's eyes dramatically showed where Murphy had shot him the previous day. He reached into his vest pocket and pulled out a dodger. He held the Wanted poster alongside the face of the corpse for comparison, and went as pale as the corpse.

'Holy shit!'

'Marshal Murphy,' the Reverend Clark intoned, 'I'll have you know that I intend to raise this act of desecration with the town council, and—'

'Oh, shove it up your ass, Reverend,' Murphy snapped.

The marshal hurried back down the hill to the town. Hal Larkin, Murphy's deputy, intercepted the Eagle Junction lawman. 'What's got you so all-fired up, Abie?' Larkin wanted to know.

The marshal swept past. Larkin was caught between the outraged mourners and the snarling marshal. Seeing that he'd have to deal with Murphy more than he would with the mourners, decided the deputy's course of action. He hared after the marshal, only catching him up as he stormed into the law office. He watched, confused, as Murphy gathered together his personal belongings, and then played catch-up to the clapboard marshal's residence at the south end of Main, still trying to find out what was bugging Abie Murphy. Valise packed and horse saddled, Hal Larkin found out when the marshal handed him the dodger that had drained the blood from his face. Larkin scratched a stubbled chin. 'Looks kinda familiar, Abie. Ain't he the fella you plugged yesterday?'

Then, like Abie Murphy when he compared the dead man to the wanted poster, the blood also drained from Hal Larkin's face. The poster read:

BEN GALT
WANTED DEAD OR ALIVE FOR MURDER,
RAPE AND BANK ROBBERY.

'Came in the noon mail,' Murphy said.

'You shot a Galt, Abie,' Larkin whined.

'Didn't know he was a Galt, did I?'

Larkin shook his head. 'Why, killing Ben Galt, Abie, you might as well have put a gun to your head. Jack Galt and his brother were closer than Satan and mortal sin,' the deputy pronounced in the doomsday tone of an Old Testament prophet. 'Jack Galt'll come looking.' The deputy continued in an even gloomier tone, 'Used to be three brothers. Jack's the only one left now. You killed Ben, and a bank guard killed Simon Galt in a town down near the border a couple years 'go. Jack and Ben Galt burned down the town in reprisal. Killed a lotta folk doing it.'

'Tell me something I don't know,' the marshal ranted.

'What're you going to do, Abie?'

'That's a dumb question, Hal. I'm hitting the trail, of course. Don't aim to sit around here waiting for Jack Galt to skin me alive, that's for sure!'

'You're lighting out? But you can't, Abie. You're the darn marshal.'

'Was the darn marshal,' the lawman grunted. Murphy ripped the star from his shirt and tossed it to Larkin. 'Congratulations, Hal. You've just been promoted.'

Hal Larkin's eyes shone. 'Me? Marshal of Eagle Junction?' But their shine was short lived, when the real meaning of being the law in Eagle Junction in the near future sank in. He looked at the star in his hand as if it were a wriggling rattler.

By now word had spread about Abie Murphy's act of desecration, and folks' blood was up. Many outrageous things happened in a Western town, but the golden rule was that when a man was dead the slate was wiped clean and due respect given. A hurriedly convened town delegation was on its way to the marshal's office to voice their disapproval of Murphy's actions, but found the marshal eating up ground out of town.

Just arriving in town, Ned Billings was forced to take urgent action to avoid Murphy's frantic charge. 'Who set fire to that critter's tail?' he enquired of an onlooker, who was every bit as bemused as Billings was.

Seconds later, Hal Larkin burst through the livery gates and hared after Abie Murphy.

'Has this place got plague?' Billings wanted to know.

Risking life and limb, the leader of the town delegation stepped into the street to bring Larkin's horse to a rearing halt. 'Where are you and the marshal headed to in such a hurry, Hal?' he questioned, curious about the sleeve of a nightshirt poking from Larkin's hastily packed valise.

'Don't know,' Hal Larkin flung back, grabbing the reins back from the delegation leader, 'but I figure that any place is going to be healthier than this burg when Jack Galt finds out that Abie planted his brother Ben.'

'Murphy killed Ben Galt?' the delegation collectively wailed.

The deputy whined, 'That means that Jack Galt'll be coming this way looking for revenge.'

Billings told the bemused onlooker, 'Ain't no place in God's creation that a man can hide from Jack Galt.'

Ned Billings rode on along Main, his gaze becoming keener as he drew nearer the general store where Dan Straker was loading a buckboard.

'Wonder what all the commotion's about, Dan?' Arthur Flint the store owner pondered.

His mind tussling with his own problems, like a second dry season, Straker had paid little heed to the happenings at the other end of the street. He shrugged, and began settling the supplies.

Flint shifted uneasily. 'Dan, I hate to bring this up. But—'

Anticipating the storekeeper's announcement, Straker handed him a thin roll of dollars, not near enough to meet his debt. 'One good crop is all I need, Arthur.'

Flint looked to the copper, cloudless sky. He tossed the feather light roll of bills in his palm. 'Not a drop of rain up there, Dan.'

Dan Straker's worried blue eyes searched the sky. 'It's got to come soon, Arthur.'

'Without rain, Dan . . .' the storekeeper clucked, and flicked the bills.

'It *will* rain soon,' Straker said with dogged insistence. 'I feel it in my bones.'

'You've got queer bones. 'Cause no one else is feeling a twinge.'

Straker pleaded, 'I need time, and credit, Arthur.'

The storekeeper looked at the goods in the buckboard, and then at the dollar bills in his hand. 'This doesn't even cover what you've loaded up, Dan. Fact is, I've got to pay for those goods, and if you don't pay me . . . well, it's not complicated to understand.' He raised his hand to stall Dan Straker's plea. 'You need water to grow crops, Dan. And with this drought looking likely to continue . . . .' He shook his head.

'To get water I need to divert that mountain stream on my western boundary, Arthur. Only that takes money I haven't got.'

'Have you talked to Saul Jennings at the bank?'

Dan Straker smiled cynically. 'The thing about banks, Arthur, is that you have to have money to get money.'

'You've got the deed of your farm as collateral.'

'Jennings wasn't impressed.' Impersonating the bank president's deep voice, Straker intoned, 'A farm without crops as collateral, is about as useful as a needle without thread for darning.'

Dan's impersonation of the banker brought a moment of light relief to the proceedings, but the gloomy content of their discussion soon re-established itself.

'You could sell the south valley, I suppose,' the storekeeper suggested. 'Sam Burns has been eyeing that valley for a long time.'

'That's my best land, Arthur. A crop will grow fastest there when—'

'I know. The rains come.'

'Truth be told, Arthur, without the south valley there isn't much merit to the farm.'

'In that case, Dan,' Flint raised hopeless hands in the air, 'you're carting your last load.'

The commotion along the street was getting more agitated by the second. Hal Larkin broke free of the crowd, and thundered out of town. The storekeeper, seeing a way out of an awkward situation, grabbed it, and hurried away.

'Best find out what that's all about, Dan.'

Dan Straker's temper flared, but he curbed his outburst. He could have no complaints, Flint had carried him for longer than most. His attention scattered, Dan was unaware of Ned Billings, scrutiny.

'Mornin', Mr Straker,' a young boy running past, greeted Dan.

'Morning to you, Billy,' Dan answered pleasantly.

'Gee, Mr Straker,' the boy said wide-eyed, 'folk are sayin' that the marshal shot Ben Galt.'

'Ben Galt?' Dan asked quietly, but keenly. 'You sure about that, Billy?'

'It's what folk are sayin', Mr Straker.'

Ned Billings watched as concern shadowed Dan Straker's face. He grinned. 'Straker, huh? Well now,' he murmured, turning to enter the saloon, 'ain't it a small world.'

Dan Straker, on board the buckboard and turning for home, thought there was something familiar about the gait of the man entering the Silver Arrow saloon.

CHAPTER TWO

On his way home, troubled by brooding thoughts, Dan Straker paused by the mountain stream which, if diverted, could turn the arid dust he was trying to coax a crop from, to the kind of rich soil that would make him a good income and bring relief from the futile toil that Mary, his wife, deserved. Drearily, he noticed that the stream had lost a lot of its volume, and maybe diverting it might not solve his problems. The long stretch to his farm over thirsty soil would soak up a lot of the water, and even if by some miracle he managed to get funding for the diversion of the stream, there was no way he could come up with the money for ducting to overcome the problem of loss through soakage. He scooped up a handful of water and watched it sparkle like diamonds, and murmured, 'Hell, I'd do almost anything!'

Mary had not spoken yet about giving up, but more and more her thoughts showed in her weary eyes. When first seen, fresh after a couple of seasonal storms, the land looked like the garden of Eden to them, tired and spent as they were from picking up the pieces after the War – Dan's loss all the greater for being on the losing side.

Their first crop, after good rainfall, fulfilled that initial promise. However, subsequent yields proved as false as the devil's promises, and the rains as fickle as the moods of a jealous heart. The earth became parched and dry; the topsoil blew away on the wind, leaving behind a brittle earth that was miserly with its bounty.

Soon, Dan Straker would have to take a decision on whether to leave or persist. Given the options, it would seem to be an easy decision to make, but walking away from a dream, even one that seemed hopeless, did not come easy. He had heard of free land in Montana, but it would likely be cow range instead of farming land, and the last thing he wanted was for Mary to have to endure a battle between sodbuster and rancher; a battle that was usually won by the cash-rich cattle barons.

Burdened, he climbed back on the buckboard and resumed his journey. Mary, as always, came from the house to meet him. It pained Dan to see how hard times had robbed her of the radiance she had had when he had first set eyes on her seven years previously, waking from an operation on his right leg smashed by a Union bullet.

'Rest easy, soldier,' she had said, softly. Dan had foggily realized that Mary was wearing the uniform of a Union nurse. 'Your war is over.'

'It's not over until the last man in grey is dead, ma'am,' he'd retorted spiritedly.

'Ma'am,' Mary had laughed. It was at that moment he had fallen hopelessly in love with her. 'I'm not sure if I like the sound of that, soldier boy.' Mary pushed him back onto the bed from which he was trying to raise himself, grimacing in pain. 'Rest, soldier,' she said, and told him with a quiet kindness. 'The South has surrendered.'

A spirited rebuff of her statement sprang to his lips, but he chewed it off. No soldier wants to believe that a war is lost; that the carnage, blood-letting and sacrifice was for nothing. However, Dan Straker had known that with losses piling up, and with the South's economy in tatters, it was only a matter of time before the Union triumphed, dogged as their resistance was. Realizing that this kind-hearted, red-haired nurse, with the most dazzling hazel eyes he had ever seen was not josh-ing him, he impulsively grabbed her hands in his and wept unashamedly.

She had returned to his bedside many times during a long and despair-filled night, sometimes to sit quietly, other times to talk in a hushed whis-per about the great future that lay ahead for all Americans.

'I'm not so sure about that,' he had doubted. 'There'll be a legacy of bitterness.'

'Oh, fiddly,' Mary had dismissed. 'I just know

that when the dust settles, men of sound sense and good heart will take this great land by the scruff of the neck, and make it the envy of the world.'

For a brief moment, Nurse Mary Duff convinced him that a miracle, because that was what it would take to heal the bleeding scars of the Civil War, was possible. But he knew that she painted a world that she wished for, rather than the world that would have to be lived in, and it was as he suspected. Rancour and bitterness were never far away, and hatred poisoned hearts were slow to give up their grudges and bitterness. Time would heal, as it always did, but before that time came many men would die still fighting a war which had long ago been lost or won.

'You'll come stay at my house, of course,' Mary had said, when there were more injured than there were nurses, doctors or beds for. 'Until that leg of yours is fully healed.'

'It'll be fine.'

'No it won't,' Mary had insisted. 'That wound is clean now, and will remain clean with care; the kind of care it won't get if you go stubbornly riding off to nowhere, Dan Straker. Which,' she added uncompromisingly, 'I'm not going to let you do!'

Two burly attendants had grabbed hold of him and carried him to a waiting barouche.

'Are you kidnapping me, Nurse Duff?' Dan had playfully joked, his heart racing at the prospect of spending time he had not been counting on in Mary's presence.

'Call it what you will, Dan Straker,' she had trumpeted, climbing on board the barouche and setting out at a steady and careful pace with his right leg cushioned by pillows. 'I'll be as careful as I can, but,' she grinned, 'you boys tore up this road good and proper in the last days of the war.' Coming to a stream which had to be crossed over a bank of rocks, Mary declared, 'And there used to be a bridge here before a Reb shell blew it to smithereens.'

Though the journey up to that point had been relatively pain-free, crossing over the rocky stream bed was not so.

'Hah!' Mary scoffed, when Dan cried out. 'And you were the one who was going to ride out on horseback. A fine mess that would have put you in.'

She stopped at the far side of the stream to check his wound, and settled the pillows under his leg with gentle hands. Her eyes, when she looked up at him, were as warm as a winter fire.

'What'll your folks say when you arrive home with a Reb, Mary?' he asked, curiously.

She thought for a moment, and then said, 'My ma will bake you an apple pie, I reckon. And my pa will get you out of that Reb uniform and into one of his suits, which will be several sizes too big for you because he's a man of sizeable girth.' Her

21

eyes clouded. 'And my brother, Tommy, won't like you one little bit, because he lost his legs at Shiloh.'

They sat together for a long quiet spell, before Dan took Mary in his arms and kissed her. She huffed and puffed, telling him that she was immune to Southern charm. But the second time he kissed her, her kiss was full and passionate, and her embrace was warm and inviting. Then they continued on, with not a single word spoken between them until they reached the house. Before going inside, Mary asked, 'What now, Dan?'

Mary's eyes joyously took in the supplies on the buckboard. 'Arthur Flint has a good heart, Dan,' she said, her hands running over the sacks of flour and cartons of dried goods, before a frown of worry took over. 'Was Arthur pleased with what you gave him?'

'Sure he was,' Dan lied, seeing no point in adding to Mary's woes.

'It'll rain soon, won't it Dan?'

'A real deluge, Mary,' he said, leaping from the buckboard with the kind of jaunty gait a man facing good times would have. 'Then this place will be greener than shamrock.'

He hugged Mary to him, and for a moment she dared to dream. She stepped back from him, the fleeting hope in her hazel eyes dying. Quietly she said, 'You wash up. I'll set the table.'

Dan watched her go to the house, his heart constricted. What had he done to the vibrant and beautiful woman whose question he had answered seven years previously.

'If you're willing,' he had said to her on the porch of her home, 'once this gammy stump of mine is working again, we could head out West, I guess. Kingdoms they say, can be built out there.'

'Oh, Dan,' she had murmured, snuggled in his arms, 'I'm surely willing.'

It had taken time to reach what he thought would be his kingdom, odd jobbing along the way to keep body and soul together, and for a spell using the gun skills he had learned in the war in his job as the marshal of a border town called Quido. There, he had honed his skills further, until his gun cleared leather lightning quick. Then one day, Mary, sensible woman that she was, had pointed out to him his growing love for a gun.

'Let's move on, Dan,' she had pleaded with him.

He had argued that a steady wage was better than scraping a living, but Mary had argued back that it was not, if it was money earned from another man's demise. The passioned intensity of her exhortations to quit his badge finally won him over, and they had moved on.

Again, Dan Straker looked to the cloudless sky and the burning horizon with not a hint of rain, and came to the decision which he had fought against making. He would sell the south valley, get what little belongings they had together, and leave for Montana.

CHAPTER THREE

The smoke in the Silver Arrow saloon was thick, but the choking smog came secondary to the worry and fear which had gripped Eagle Junction since they had learned of Ben Galt's death.

'Running scared bastard!' was the general opinion of Abie Murphy's hurried departure.

Each man in the saloon added to the list of the Galt gang's atrocities, some true, some rumour and hearsay, but even if a tenth of what was told was correct, then Eagle Junction was looking into hell itself. Many men had tried to nail the Galts – Jack Galt in particular, figuring that if you cut off the head of the monster then its other parts would wither too, but all had failed. Now, everyone who bucked Galt, through ignorance or stupidity (because they were the only reasons left why a man should do so), just ran for as long as they could until Jack Galt caught up with them. His blood-spattered history proved that he always did.

'Murphy took what was in the law office safe with

him,' Charlie Gant, the keeper of the town purse grumbled. 'Every nickel.'

'Blasted Ben Galt when he was skunk drunk, too,' the round-shouldered livery owner said, presumably offering this as evidence of Abie Murphy's scurillous nature.

'Now what kind of cur shoots a man when he's skunk drunk?' another man added.

'Yeah. Sure shows what kind of snake Murphy was,' the blackjack dealer at the Silver Arrow put in, grabbing his chance to bad-mouth the marshal for the times he'd slung him in jail for dealing from a crooked deck.

'Can't recall anyone protesting when Marshal Murphy shot Ben Galt.'

All eyes, glaring hotly, shot towards the man sitting at a table behind the angry crowd. The livery owner was the first to overcome his anger and speak, vigorously challenging the man with the goatee beard. 'Are you taking Murphy's side, Doc?'

'No.'

'Then what the heck are ya doin, Doc?' a fiery-haired man with a red, Irish complexion asked, his fists already balling for a fight.

'Just making an observation of how you gents didn't mind what tactics Murphy employed when you wanted him to rid you of a problem. Doesn't seem fair now, leastways to me, that you should condemn him when you condoned him.'

'Ben Galt was raising hell,' the livery owner reminded Doc Whitley.

A chorus of *yeahs* went up.

Unfazed, Whitley went on, 'Maybe if some of you fellas had crawled out from under your beds or from behind your women's skirts to help Murphy, he might not have had to shoot Galt at all, and we wouldn't have a problem that's too big for this town to handle.'

The town council chairman piped up, 'That's a mite unfair, Doc. None of us were gun-skilled enough to face up to Ben Galt. Besides, that's what we paid Abie Murphy good dollars for.'

'Ain't we gettin' 'head of ourselves?' All eyes went to Lucky Dando, the owner of the Silver Arrow saloon.

'What d'ya mean, Lucky?' a gambler at the interrupted game of blackjack, asked.

'Well, maybe Jack Galt will never find out 'bout his brother's demise,' the saloon owner elaborated.

'That's clutching at straws, Lucky,' the livery owner flung back.

It was an opinion that Charles Wayne, the town lawyer, agreed with. 'Galt will hear all right. Saw that gent who came to sit on the hotel porch about the same time that Ben Galt put in an appearace leaving town yesterday, shortly after Abie Murphy shot Galt.' The lawyer, as lawyers do, stood up and occupied the centre of the floor. 'I'd bet my

27

bottom dollar that that gent was Ben Galt's back-up man.'

'Back-up man?' the livery owner yelped.

'Not much of a back-up, if you ask me,' the town blacksmith grunted. 'Seein' that Ben Galt is now wormbait.'

Charles Wayne said, 'I think Ben Galt was here for a purpose.'

'What purpose would that be, Charles?' Saul Jennings, Eagle Junction's banker asked, figuring that he already knew the answer; an answer that made the normally unflappable bank president sweat.

'I figure that Ben Galt was here to size up the bank and test our mettle. Only he got a mite too fond of whores and whiskey, and got careless enough to draw on Abie Murphy when he was probably seeing four of him. I reckon that the Galt gang is just across the border in Mexico, waiting for Ben Galt to report back.'

An old-timer, with only a solitary tooth, laughed. 'Well their asses are goin' to wear mighty thin if they're waitin' for Ben Galt to put in an 'pear-ance.'

The old-timer's infectious laughter brought brief relief to the dour proceedings, before Charles Wayne brought the pall back.

'When Jack Galt hears about his brother's death in this town, no man, woman or child will be safe.'

Heads went down.

'Has anyone got an answer to our predicament?'

The question was Arthur Flint's.

Ned Billings, who had been quietly nursing a whiskey at the bar, answered, 'I might have.'

All eyes went the stranger's way.

'Might have?' Flint probed.

Billings nodded. 'Reckon so, mister.'

Since he had learned of Eagle Junction's dilemma, and had seen the man whom he knew as Josh Lawson, but who the town knew as Dan Straker, Ned Billings had begun to see a way to fill his depleted pockets before moving on. He had planned a short stay in town to see if there were rich pickings; however, with Jack Galt on the way, Eagle Junction would be a decidedly unhealthy place to hang around.

'Go on, sir,' Flint urged Billings.

Billings smiled slyly. 'How about me and a couple of the town's more prosperous citizens getting together to talk,' he suggested to Flint.

'Why would you wanna do that, stranger?' the blacksmith enquired, miffed.

'Agreed, sir,' Saul Jennings said, recognizing an opening gambit with a banker's shrewdness. He stood up. 'Might I suggest the bank as an appropriate meeting place?'

Billings grinned. 'Suits me dandy, mister.'

'Thought it might,' Jennings snorted.

CHAPTER FOUR

Seated in Jennings' office at the bank were Arthur Flint, Charles Wayne, and Sam Levridge, one of Eagle Junction's wealthiest men. They waited for the dusty stranger to state how he could help them. Billings, who from long experience knew how to heighten expectations to the point of desperation, selected one of Saul Jennings' fine Havana cigars which did not please the banker, as the expensive smokes were reserved for the bank's more prestigious clientele. He fired up the smoke with tantalizing slowness and infinite pleasure, and then took several long drags of the weed before beginning, 'Well, now, gentlemen, I reckon that Josh Lawson could be yours and this town's saviour.'

'Josh Lawson?' Levridge asked, in a whine of a voice that was completely at odds with his bulky frame. 'Who the hell's Josh Lawson, mister?'

'Josh Lawson,' Ned Billings said, 'is one of the fastest guns I've ever seen. But . . . .' He left them hanging on his words until they were ready to leap from their chairs to throttle him. 'More important still, is that Josh Lawson might be the only man Jack Galt will listen to. Or . . . .' He let the seconds tick by, enjoying his audience's discomfort. 'If necessary, the only man that would stand a chance of killing Galt.'

'Talk to Jack Galt?' Arthur Flint snorted, derisively.

Billings explained, 'Josh Lawson once saved Jack Galt's life. Took a bullet in the leg doing so. Busted it. Now, the fact is, that Jack Galt mightn't care a fig nowdays about Lawson's act of bravery – Galt's dropped a long way from being a Southern gentleman, and that's where Lawson's prowess with a gun comes in.'

'How is all this going to help us now, Mr Billings?' Saul Jennings wanted to know. 'The Galt gang will have burned this town long before Lawson can get here.'

Ned Billings' grin was as wide as the Rio Grande. 'The next piece of information is going to cost you gents,' he said.

'Cost us?' Levridge squeaked.

'One thousand dollars, that's what I figure it's worth,' Billings gloated.

'A thous—' Flint choked.

Charles Wayne said in a calm tone of voice, 'Are you going to sell us the map to El Dorado, Mr Billings?'

'Good as, I reckon,' Billings said cockily. 'A thousand dollars is chicken feed to save your hides, gents.'

Eyes met, and Saul Jennings said, 'A thousand dollars it is, Mr Billings.'

Ned Billings held out his hand. The bank president took a safe box from his desk drawer and counted out ten one hundred dollar bills.

'Let's hear what's worth so darn much,' Levridge groused, sounding like the air escaping from a wheezing bellows.

Billings told them, 'Josh Lawson is right here on your doorstep, gents.'

'In Eagle Junction?' Arthur Flint quizzed.

'Yep. Saw him less than an hour ago, right out there in the street, large as life. Only you fellas know him as Dan Straker.'

Their gaping mouths closed, Billings went on to tell them about how he served for a brief spell of madness as Josh Lawson's deputy, and then headed for the door. 'Guess I'll be on my way now, gents.'

A Colt .45 being cocked stopped Billings in his tracks. He turned slowly to look at the holder of the gun. Saul Jennings said, 'Used to have this in the safe. Always scared me to look at it. Ugly, isn't it? Had a notion that one day I would open the safe and this would go off. Luckily I changed it for a derringer just this morning.' Chillingly, he told Billings, 'I think you should accept the hospitality of the town jail, Mr Billings. Just until we check out your story.'

'Fast thinking, Saul,' Arthur Flint complimented the banker.

Billings sighed. 'Don't be long about it, gents. I want to be long gone before Jack Galt comes a-calling.'

CHAPTER FIVE

Mary Straker watched her thoughtful husband across the dinner table. 'What is it, Dan?' she asked. 'You've not sat easy since you came back from town.'

He smiled. 'Sometimes it's a real cross to be married to a watchful woman.' He looked her steady in the eye. 'Abie Murphy shot Ben Galt.'

'Is that all? I reckon he had it coming, Dan. Him and Jack, both.'

'Is that all? Isn't that enough? Jack Galt will likely raze Eagle Junction to the ground.'

Mary said, 'Jack Galt's surely got the spite in him to do just that.'

Mary Straker's mind went back to the rainy night when Dan had been delivered into her care at the field hospital, assisted by Jack Galt whose life he had just saved, which was the reason for his broken leg.

'Maybe you shouldn't have stopped that bullet meant for Jack Galt, Dan,' she opined. 'It would have saved a whole lot of folk a whole lot of trouble since.' Shrewdly, she sized up her husband. 'But I'm betting that Jack Galt isn't your main concern. It's Arthur Flint, isn't it?'

With a resigned sigh, Straker told her, 'Flint says that what was in the buckboard today is all there's going to be until I pay what I owe.'

Mary Straker said desperately, 'But you paid him what you could, Dan.'

'A hundred and fifty dollars against a bill of over five hundred isn't much, Mary.'

'But you're good for the rest when we'll get a crop. Doesn't Arthur understand that?'

'I reckon he does.'

'So?'

'So it isn't much use him understanding, if my bill keeps mounting. Because his suppliers won't understand if he can't pay what he owes.'

Mary Straker pushed her plate aside and angrily jumped up from the table. 'When times were good, Flint took your money, Dan.'

'And I got the goods in return, honey.'

Sudden, weary tears welled up in Mary Straker's eyes. 'Without supplies, we're finished here, Josh.'

'Don't call me by that name!'

Defiantly, she said, 'I like it better than Dan. Anyway, what harm can it do to call you Josh when we're alone?'

'We agreed that when we left Quido behind, we'd change our names. You've got to call me Dan,

36

Mary – all the time. Otherwise, if you call me Josh in private, it'll only be a matter of time before you'll slip up and call me Josh in public.' Moderating his tone, he continued, 'I've changed in the last couple of years. Got older – more worn. But there are still people around who, if they heard you call me Josh, might just remember who I am. The last thing we need is for some buck building a reputation to come looking for me.' He concluded, dourly: 'No one must know who I really am, Mary.'

Straker took his wife in his arms and held her tightly to him, his heart breaking at the sound of her sobbing. He stroked her red hair until her sobbing eased.

'Are we finished, Dan?'

Resolutely, he said, 'We're not finished by a long shot, Mary.'

Brief hope flared in her eyes. 'You have a plan?' she asked, her spirits leaping.

'Sure I do.'

Euphorically, she asked, 'What plan, Dan?'

'I'm going to sell the south valley.'

'Sell the south valley,' Mary yelped. Deflated, she groaned, 'That's your sure-fire survival plan?'

Irked by her attitude, Dan flung back, 'It's better than your plan, which is no plan at all!' And seeing the hurt well up in her eyes again, he enfolded her in his arms. 'Oh, heck, honey, the one thing that's always seen us through hard times was our common purpose.' He held her at arm's length. 'Lose that, and no plan at all will be any good.'

Mary Straker kissed her husband gently, and then said, sensibly, 'Without the south valley, Dan, this farm isn't worth a sack of beans.'

Of course, Straker knew this to be true, but he still persisted that with their debts cleared they could survive without the valley. He failed to convince Mary.

'Might as well face the truth we've been hiding from, Dan. There's going to be no rain, no crop, and no farm.'

'The money I'll get for the south valley will be enough to divert the mountain stream,' Dan enthused. 'In no time at all, this whole place will have crops so tall that the sun will have to go round if it wants to pass.'

'Times are hard. What do you think you'll get for the valley, Dan?'

'Oh, I reckon fifteen hundred, maybe some more.'

'The only buyer is Sam Burns. With a range full of hollow-siders, I don't see how he can.'

'Sam is the wealthiest man in the territory.' Adamantly, Dan insisted, 'I reckon that Sam will settle for near enough to what I'm asking. He's been eyeing that valley long enough.'

Mary Straker was shaking her head, the way she might with a wayward child.

'What now?' Straker asked, tetchily.

'This drought has given everyone problems, Dan. Right now, with things so bad all round, Sam Burns just might not have the cash to buy the valley.'

In his desperation, Dan had not allowed himself to be downcast, but Mary's considered reasoning forced hard reality on him. It was as she said, of course, the drought was a curse on every man's house. Dan grabbed his hat and headed for the door.

'There's only one sure way to find out,' he said. 'That's ask Sam Burns straight out.'

He was halfway across the yard when Mary caught him up. 'Maybe you should give this some more thought, Dan,' she urged. 'That valley was our hope of making something half decent of this place.'

'That's not necessarily so, Mary,' Dan argued. 'Once that mountain stream is diverted—'

Mary interjected, 'Without the valley, no matter how much darn water this place gets, it won't be worth working. We'll break our backs for little or nothing, and you know that.'

'No, I don't know that,' Straker said stubbornly, and strode off to the barn to saddle his horse.

Mary thought about going after him, but knew from long experience that her husband, once he got a bone to chew on, would keep right on chewing until cold reality brought him to his senses. She could have no complaints, she told herself. It was that kind of dogged drive that had first attracted her to Josh Lawson, as she'd always think of him. Now, with some regret, she thought about how she might have done more to have persuaded Dan to accept her father's offer of partnership, when all the objections he had raised to their marriage had gone unheeded. Her brother, Tommy, legless, would be no help to her father except in little ways, like keeping the books right and doing some odd chores that could be done from an invalid chair. But, of course, she knew then as she did now, that Tommy would never have accepted Dan. He had years of bitterness ahead, and a Confederate shell to blame for it.

'I'd prefer to share a roof with Satan himself than a damn Reb,' had been Tommy's bitter response to her father's suggestion. 'If Lawson moves in, I move out!'

'Tommy will come round, Dan,' Mary had argued. 'He's hot-blooded now, but in time he'll cool.'

Dan's reply had ended all discussion on the matter. 'I'm moving on, Mary. Time for you to choose.'

There was no choice to make, Josh Lawson owned her heart. Oh, there were times when she might have had some regret, what woman hadn't. But her keenest regret was in not being able to give Dan a child. Other than that she would not have changed much, if anything, in the years she had been Josh Lawson's wife – Dan Straker's wife, she mentally corrected herself. Dan was right, she must stop thinking of him as Josh Lawson, or else one day her foolish tongue would reveal who Dan really was.

'A fast gun attracts trouble, Mary,' he had explained, when he had shed his star. 'There's always someone looking to be faster.'

'Pretty yourself up, woman,' Dan said, riding past. 'There's a barn dance in town tonight, and this time we'll be able to afford more than one glass of punch between us.'

Sure, she'd pretty herself up, and doing so was no small effort these days. They might even go to the dance, but, she reckoned, they would still be sharing one glass of punch.

As Dan made tracks to Sam Burns, Arthur Flint arrived from town.

'Hello, Arthur,' Mary greeted the storekeeper, her earlier anger abated. Flint had been tolerant of their debt, and deserved merit for that.

Flint asked, 'Dan around?'

'Just left. Headed over to see Sam Burns.'

'Burns?'

'Yeah. Dan's decided to sell him the south valley.'

'Never!'

'You know better than most that we've been bucking the odds, Arthur. The thing is that the odds have been bucking back even harder still.'

'Diverting that stream might just work, Mary,' Flint opined.

Mary Straker looked about the dust-blown yard and fields beyond. She smiled sadly. 'Maybe it will at that, Arthur.' Returning her gaze to the store-keeper, she said, 'You're welcome to step inside until Dan gets back.'

'Maybe I'll catch Dan up before he reaches the Burns ranch.'

Mary laughed. 'On the nag he's on, I figure snails will pass him out.'

As he rode away, Flint drew rein momentarily. 'You know, Mary. Maybe you'll have that water and get to keep the valley, too.'

Brows furrowed in puzzlement, Mary Straker watched Arthur Flint into the distance. 'Now, Julius,' she asked the cat, picking him up on her way back inside the house, 'what do you suppose that was all about?'

Julius purred.

'Oh, that's it, huh?'

Mary hugged the cat to her and sighed. Again, she looked across the dust-blown yard to the sky beyond. A single cloud was not normally some-thing to get excited about, but now Mary's heart leaped on seeing it drift lazily along the horizon. Her lips moved in a silent prayer.

CHAPTER SIX

On walking into the cantina and seeing the four cut-throats drinking with Jack Galt, Ike Cramer regretted not having made tracks for the Canadian wilderness, instead of walking into what might prove to be his demise, should Galt consider that his healthy arrival in Mexico might be a sign of a lack of committment to Ben Galt's survival. Cramer consoled himself with the thought that, even if he had headed for the Canadian wilderness, on some far-off day Jack Galt would arrive on his doorstep. Galt was feared for his loathsome deeds, but he was more feared for his relentless pursuit of revenge against those who earned his wrath.

Jack Galt's gaze went beyond Ike Cramer to the cantina door, clearly expecting Ben Galt to be on Cramer's tail. When he was not, his gaze returned to Cramer, and his features set in stone.

'B-bad news, J-Jack,' Cramer stammered, his gut curling with fear.

*

Arthur Flint cursed on seeing Sam Burns greet and escort Dan Straker into the ranch house. There were a couple of trails which led to the Burns ranch, and he had unluckily chosen the wrong one. Being a townie, his knowledge of the country was not on par with Straker's, and that ignorance of the terrain had worked against him. Now, the money him and his partners had paid Ned Billings might be money wasted, if Sam Burns bought the south valley from Dan Straker. However, Flint consoled himself, Burns like everyone else was suffering from the drought, so his cash reserves were probably lower as a result and he might not be able to buy the valley. Or, maybe, he could hope, that even if Sam Burns bought the valley, Dan Straker would still be open to going back on the deal if him and his partners raised the figure they had agreed on to offer Straker for the task of trying to stave off Jack Galt's revenge on Eagle Junction. But as soon as that thought came to mind, Flint rejected it. Dan Straker was an honest dealing man. If he struck a deal with Sam Burns, then that would be that. There would be no going back on it, irrespective of what inducement he might offer.

'Place your best feature right there, Dan,' Sam Burns invited, indicating a plushly upholstered chair that was a left-over from when the Burns ranch was in healthy profit, before the drought struck. 'Whiskey?' He held up a decanter from the drinks cabinet in his den, and chuckled. 'Kentucky. Should go down smooth in a Johnny Reb.'

Dan Straker took no offence. Sam Burns, though a distinguished Union colonel before he took to nursing cows, was the most tolerant man of another man's views that he had come across since the end of the war. He laughed along with the rancher.

'Nice to see that an old reprobate Yank can tell good whiskey from that rotgut swill you fellas usually guzzle.'

Burns poured, and then came to sit in a chair alongside Dan Straker. 'What can I do for you, Dan?'

'You've done plenty as it is,' Straker said, and it was the truth. 'I couldn't have held out this long without your neighbourliness, Sam.'

The rancher placed a hand on Dan's shoulder. 'We're all at the mercy of this damn drought, Dan.' He sighed heavily. 'Some days I feel like getting on my horse and leaving it all behind.'

'I understand the feeling, Sam.'

They sipped their whiskies for a while, each man with his own thoughts. It was Sam Burns who broke the impasse.

'You're here to sell me the south valley, aren't you, Dan?'

Dan Straker nodded. 'You buying, Sam?'

'Not for what you've got in mind, I dare say. It's a fine valley, if somewhat dejected right now.' He pondered. 'If I was doing the selling, I'd be asking for . . . oh, two thousand dollars, I reckon.'

'Fifteen hundred.'

'A bargain,' Burns said.

After a moment, Dan asked, 'So, why aren't you grabbing, Sam?'

'Nothing to grab with.' He hunched his shoulders. 'Time was that I'd go to that safe right behind that picture there.' He pointed to a painting of a bucking mustang. 'I'd reach in and take fifteen hundred dollars out and gladly hand it over for the ownership of the south valley, and reckon that I'd got m'self a bargain.'

He stood up and rambled about the den, before going to the safe to open it.

'But there's more dust than cash in this iron box now, Dan.' He turned back to Straker. 'I've got cows dropping. Grass that's turned to straw, and dry creeks. I've been lucky that I dug that well out back a couple of years ago, but there isn't near enough water in it to water the herd, even reduced as it has been, and its yielding less by the day to boot. Soon, if rain doesn't come, all that well will be giving will be water for the house, and I'll be lucky if that holds out.'

He came back to sit alongside Straker.

'I'm sorry, Dan. Right now I couldn't afford a

hundred dollars for the south valley.' Then, brightening, 'Anyway, you'll want that valley when the rains come.'

Dourly, Dan said, 'The rains aren't coming.' He stood up and walked to the door. 'At least not in time for me. Thanks for the hospitality you've shown me, and the help you've given me, Sam.'

Burns looked at him steadily. 'Sounds like you're getting ready to quit, Dan?'

Straker's weariness took in every inch of him. 'Can't see what else there is to do, Sam. Other than pray for a miracle.'

'Miracles happen, Dan. Sometimes.'

Ike Cramer wilted under Jack Galt's glare. He was the sweatiest Americano in all of Mexico. 'Nothin' I could do, Jack,' he grovelled. 'Ben wouldn't listen to nothin' I had to say.'

An old clock behind the cantina bar ticked the seconds off – each tick, to Cramer's ears, sounding like another nail being hammered in the lid of his coffin. Funny, he'd been in the cantina at least a hundred times over the years, and this was the first time he had noticed the clock.

Raul Sanchez, the only Mexican in the Galt gang (because Jack Galt hated Mexicans every bit as much as Negroes), stood up. He was the closest to a friend Jack Galt had. In fact the only company that Jack Galt liked being in was Southern white company, but in Raul Sanchez, Galt had found a man as equally devoid of conscience and as ruthless as himself.

Jack Galt's black pebble eyes bore into Ike Cramer with the severity of an Indian lance. Shit, Cramer thought, why hadn't he lit out for Canada?

Sanchez's smile was wolfish. 'Ben's dead, huh, Ike?'

His tone was chillingly calm – the kind of montone voice he spoke in before cutting a man's heart from its roots. Ike Cramer's bowels rumbled. He felt like a man must feel, he reckoned, when he was helpless and vultures were waiting to rip him apart.

'Ben figured that he might as well have some fun while he was sizin' up the bank at Eagle Junction.' Desperate, Cramer pleaded, 'I tried to warn him that he was taking too much of a risk hangin' round, Jack. But he was havin' too much fun to listen.'

'Who killed him?' Jack Galt demanded to know.

'A badge-toter by the name of Abie Murphy. Gunned Ben down when he was drunk, too. The town just stood by and let it happen. Pure murder, it was, Jack.'

Sociably, Galt invited, 'Have a drink, Ike. The long ride would have made you thirsty, my friend.' One of the men handed Cramer a bottle of tequila, from which he slugged sparingly. His preference was for American whiskey, and he rated tequila no better than bathtub rotgut. 'Sit,' Galt added, sliding a chair Cramer's way.

'Mighty kind, Jack,' Cramer said, sitting. 'But,' he shook the contents of the bottle, 'think I could have me some American whiskey instead of this whore's piss.'

Jack Galt laughed. He called to the barkeep, 'Pablo. Whiskey, American, for my friend.'

Raul Sanchez, an intensely patriotic Mexican, saw no humour in the exchange.

The barkeep brought a bottle of whiskey and immediately vanished back behind the bar, taking up a position at the far end of the long bar out of range of any lead that might start flying. Cramer slugged from the whiskey bottle, creating clear glass almost quarter of the way down.

'Good, eh, Ike,' Galt said.

'Sure is, Jack.'

Jack Galt held out his hand for the bottle. Cramer handed it over. Galt added significantly to the amount of clear glass. He held out the bottle to Cramer. Ike Cramer was beginning to relax. Maybe, he was thinking, this will be OK. The outlaw reached for it, unsuspecting, and when suddenly Galt flicked the bottle and smashed it on his skull, Ike Cramer's surprise was total. A jagged wound opened up from Cramer's forehead to behind his right ear. Cramer sagged and toppled out of his chair under the blow. Jack Galt, unmoved by Cramer's moaning, followed through with a boot to Cramer's gut. Bile spewed from his mouth. Galt rubbed Ike Cramer's face in the mixture of blood and vomit, much to the amusement of the gang members sitting round the table. Raul Sanchez's amusement was the fullest of all.

Ike Cramer curled up in a futile effort to protect himself from the boots raining in from the gang members. There were other men in the cantina, but no one challenged Jack Galt, or went to Cramer's assistance. Everyone present had heard of the awful retribution Galt dealt out to any man who had tried to curb his excesses of cruelty, themselves ending up as victims of his loco rages.

'You know what, Ike,' Jack Galt, kneeling alongside Cramer, said, 'I think you ran out on Ben like a scared rabbit.' He grabbed Cramer by the hair and yanked his head back. 'For that I am going to kill you.' He leaned closer to whisper, 'Slowly.'

Sanchez's boot, delivered with venom, landed on Ike Cramer's spine. Bone snapped, and he howled out in pain.

'My legs,' he wailed. 'My legs are dead.'

'Why did you do that, Raul?' Galt sniggered. 'Now the boys'll have to carry this bundle of dogshit, 'cause he hasn't got legs to walk with any more. Outside,' he ordered. 'Feed him to the dogs.' One of the gang drew his six gun. Galt brushed it aside. 'Alive!'

Even the hardened outlaws blanched.

'What're you waiting for?'

Two of the men grabbed Ike Cramer and

dragged him outside, howling.

'Stake him out.'

'For pity's sake,' a friar hurrying from the church intervened, 'this is wrong. It is against God's will.'

'God?' Galt scoffed. 'I don't see no God, Padre.'

'Do this,' the priest said, 'and you'll burn in hell for all eternity.'

The gang leader chuckled. 'I don't think so, priest. You see, I reckon, Satan doesn't burn his friends.'

The aged friar, though shaking, stood firm. 'This you will not do, Galt!'

On hearing the priest's protest, Cyrus Hanley stepped from the cantina, aware of the danger the priest was in. The old friar was a good and kind man, and enjoyed immunity from hardcases who fled to Mexico. But Hanley reckoned that that was about to change.

'This I will not do, you say, priest?' Jack Galt's face filled with an angry hatred. 'You will stop me?' He laughed harshly. 'Or maybe this God of yours will stop me, eh, Father?'

Galt shouted out: 'Heh, God. Are you going to stop me feeding this bastard to the dogs?' He cocked and ear and listened. 'Seems to me that God's not listening, Padre.' He spun around to face his men. 'Stake Cramer out!'

The monk blocked the men's path, and courageously announced, 'I will not let you do this.'

Galt said, 'Look around, Father.' The villagers were hurrying indoors, while the men in the saloon, with the exception of Cyrus Hanley, stayed put. 'No one will help you.'

The old priest's gaze came to rest on Cyrus Hanley, a lone figure. With him he did not plead. What could one man do. A friend of Cyrus Hanley sidled up to the edge of the cantina door to urge the outlaw:

'Get back in here, Cyrus. Or Galt'll feed you to the dogs, too.'

Hanley, though an outlaw, was not one by instinct or nature. The crime which had set him on the owlhoot trail was one of desperation, rather than malice, having robbed a bank in Texas to get back what he saw as his money, when the bank was too quick to foreclose on his farm so that a crony of the bank president could grab what he had worked himself to a standstill to build.

'Get out of the way, Padre,' Jack Galt snarled.

Looking skywards, the friar intoned, 'Help me Lord to remain steadfast in your service. Do not let me weaken. Keep me safe from the snares of Satan, who is present here and now.'

'Are you going to move, Priest?' Galt grated.

Covered with the sweat of fear, Father Daniel Joseph Ryan declared, 'There will no murder here this day, Galt.' The old priest crossed himself, and his trembling lips moved in prayer.

Galt sighed, and turned away to walk back to the

cantina. For the briefest of moments, the Irish friar thought he had won the day, until Jack Galt turned, a knife flashing in his hand. The priest dropped to his knees clutching at the knife protruding from his throat, his eyes awash with pain and defeat.

Shock immobilized Cyrus Hanley.

Galt strolled to where the monk lay stricken and forced the knife deeper, until it's tip emerged from the back of the padre's neck. Jack Galt's barbarity shocked even the most hardened of the rabble gathered in the cantina, but none had the fortitude to challenge Galt. Heads went down, eyes were shut, breaths were held. It was a harsh land, with much cruelty perpetrated. It took all of a man's concentration to survive himself, without taking on board other men's troubles.

Ike Cramer was staked out. Through the long hot afternoon, Galt's men revived him many times, making another incision in his flesh with each visit to give the gathering wild dogs and other animals the scent of fresh blood. Vultures took up perches on the roofs, watching and waiting. A couple of times they got impatient and swooped down, their ugly beaks slashing at Cramer's stricken body. His attempts to scatter them grew ever weaker as the shadows of dusk lenghtened across the village. The priest's body, lying in a pool of crusted blood, was swarmed with flies and hungry insects crawling from the many holes and crevices in the rutted street. Once or twice, Cyrus Hanley almost worked up the courage to retrieve the padre's body and take it to the church, but his nerve failed him at the last second.

As darkness closed in, the watching eyes now circling the village began to glow, and the sucking of saliva-filled mouths sent Cyrus Hanley's blood running cold. Ike Cramer's moans became whimpers.

'He's dying,' Galt barked, and ordered Raul Sanchez, 'Cut his belly open. But keep him alive long enough for him to feel jaws tearing at him.'

'No man deserves to die like this,' Hanley told a couple of the men gathered on the far side of the cantina, out of Galt's hearing.

Hanley had spent the afternoon hating his own cowardice. His concern was not entirely for Ike Cramer; he was a man who had ridden with Galt and shared in his vileness. His shame was that he had not had the courage to stand with Father Ryan, who had nursed him through a fever the previous year, and had shown him and the men who now cringed in fear of Galt's anger, kindness and compassion, even though they were utterly undeserving.

'Stay out of it, Cyrus,' the man who had earlier sidled up to the cantina door warned the outlaw. 'Ain't none of your business.'

Another man, with a nose straying all over his face having had it broken time and again in saloon brawls, griped, 'You ain't got no right to get Galt all riled up and mean, Hanley.'

'Yeah,' a lanky man with a face that could be used to scare children, added, 'You gotta gripe with Galt, you make it plain that it's your gripe 'lone, mister.'

Hanley growled, 'Damn Galt! Damn us, too, for standing by and letting this happen.'

'You're leaving, friend?' Jack Galt enquired ominously, as Cyrus Hanley strode from the cantina.

'Got miles to cover.'

'In the dark?'

'I like sleeping under the stars.'

Hanley averted his gaze as he passed the blood-ied mass of Ike Cramer. A couple of yards on, he turned, walked back to where the dying man was staked out, and shot him through the head. When the echo of the gun's blast faded away, it left behind a silent, menacing void. Cyrus Hanley shook. He was not a brave man. In the main he had lived his life avoiding trouble when he could. But the evil he had witnessed, had triggered in him a decency which had been his hallmark before he had hit the owlhoot trail and been hardened by living with men who were often no better than animals.

But now, acting on emotion instead of good sense, had made him Jack Galt's enemy.

'Sorry, Padre,' he murmured as he walked past

the dead friar. 'But you'll understand, I'm sure, that hitting the trail fast must now be my priority.'

He was halfway across the street, pinching himself that he was still breathing. The livery was getting closer by the second, but it also only took a second to die. He heard the creak of the cantina door and stiffened his back for the inevitable bullet. At least that would be better than being devoured by wild dogs. That was, if Galt did not decide to make him the meal instead of Ike Cramer. The temptation to turn and start shooting was overwhelming; a kind of madness to get things over with.

He glanced to his right – the water trough. Should he dive for cover? What use would that be? Galt and his gang made five to one against, with another couple of men scattered about the village enjoying its pleasures.

'Friend!' Hanley froze. 'What if I don't want you to leave?'

Quaking, Cyrus Hanley turned slowly, levelling the .45 he still held on Jack Galt. He fought to overcome the fear in his voice and the looseness in his gut. 'If I'm not leaving, Galt, I'm sure as hell going to make certain that you stay right here with me!'

Galt scoffed. 'You're a fool, mister. You don't hold any aces.'

Hanley said, 'One bullet right in your heart, that's all it will take, Galt.'

'There are five of us.'

'Gamble if you will, Galt.'

Hanley backed towards the livery. The Mexican livery man shoved his horse through the door, unsaddled.

'Saddle it,' Hanley growled.

'Meester,' the man pleaded.

Hanley said, 'You can take a chance on Galt not killing you, Mex. But you can be sure that I will.'

On board the mare, Hanley yanked the Winchester from its scabbard and held it on Jack Galt until the darkness cloaked him. Furious with Galt's inaction, Raul Sanchez went to follow, but Galt held him back.

'Let him sweat. We'll hunt him down later.' Grimly, he concluded, 'It will be a pleasure worth waiting for, that I promise you.'

CHAPTER SEVEN

Dan Straker wasted no time in making tracks back home. He worried about Mary being alone. Of late, hungry Indians had been stealing what little Dan and his neighbours had. There had been a couple of bad-tempered skirmishes and one fatality, an old Dutch prospector who had apparently been murdered for a plate of beans, but Dan had his own opinion about Dutchy Cryuff's killing. Rumour was that Dutchy had a secret stash, and Dan believed that it was this rumour that had sealed Cryuff's fate – desperate times made for desperate deeds. Law and order, slipshod at the best of times, would, on Abie Murphy's and Hal Larkin's flight, completely break down.

Appearing suddenly from a wooded slope on a bend in the trail, Arthur Flint nearly fell foul of Straker's heightened sense of urgency.

'Whoa! Easy, Dan,' the storekeeper yelled, as Straker's Colt flashed from leather, cocked and ready.

He angrily rebuked Flint, 'That was a darn fool move to make.'

'Didn't know that your nerves were jangling that much,' Flint flung back, peeved, seeing the fault entirely as Straker's. But he had the evidence he wanted. Ned Billings was right, Dan Straker's gun, or rather Josh Lawson's gun, had cleared leather in a blink. He said, smoothly, 'Never knew you could handle a gun that slickly, Dan.'

Straker cursed his reaction. Up to now he had played the role of a slow moving sodbuster to perfection, never giving a hint of having been anything else. His problem now was, should he ignore Flint's remarks and hope that the storekeeper would forget what he had seen? Or maybe put his fast draw down to good fortune? Or should he make some glib response to try and pass off as a joke, what Flint had seen? Either approach held its dangers. Dan opted for no comment at all. He slid his six gun back into its holster and said, conversationally, 'For a man who seldom puts a foot outside of town limits, you're way off the beaten track, Arthur.'

'Is it any wonder I never stray,' the storekeeper groused, flapping at the million bugs buzzing round him.

Amused by Flint's antics, Dan said, 'I'd best get you back to the house, before those pesky bugs eat you alive, Arthur. They like storekeeper's blood, I reckon.'

Horrified, Flint examined his smooth, unblemished hands for signs of bite marks. Dan's amusement was all the greater.

'I guess those critters are just plain tired of the same old diet all the time. Let's go.'

As he led off, Flint grabbed Dan's reins. 'I'm way out here, being eaten alive, 'cause what I've got to say is not for Mary's ears, Dan. Well,' he amended, 'not right now.'

'Oh?'

A quiver of apprehension raced through Dan Straker. Was Flint about to force him to sell up to pay what he owed? He wouldn't have thought that Flint was that kind of man. But, of course, he was not the storekeeper's only defaulter, and with money becoming more scarce all the time, Flint might be panicking. There was no telling how a man in the throes of panic might act.

Shrewdly reading Dan's thoughts, Flint reassured him, 'I'm not here to bring you grief, Dan. I'm here to help you and Mary.'

Puzzled, Dan asked, 'Help? How?'

Still swatting insects, the storekeeper pleaded, 'Is there some place we can talk?' He flapped furiously. 'Before these bastards have the last drop of my blood?'

Thoughtful, Straker led the way along a narrow, winding track that led to an abandoned cabin. Once inside, Flint wasted no time in stating the reason for his visit.

'You used to be a lawman, that so?' Dan stood stock-still. His heart staggered when Flint added, 'Josh.'

Straker did not bother trying to deny his past. He could only ponder on how it had been revealed, and who had done the telling? Flint supplied the answer.

'Know a fella by the name of Ned Billings, Dan?'

Dan's mind flashed back to the man he had seen entering the Silver Arrow saloon as he was leaving town. Now he knew why his gait was familiar – he had seen it every day in Quido when Billings had been his deputy. Dan remembered Billings as a man with a larcenous and underhanded nature, which was totally unsuited to marshalling. His tenure had been short. In fact, he had run Ned Billings out of town.

'Some day, Lawson,' Billings had sworn, 'I'll even the score for this.'

He had.

'What is it you want, Arthur?' Dan asked, seeing no point in prevarication.

'Billings says that Jack Galt owes you. That you saved his life, just when a Yankee rifle was about to blow him clear to Satan's clutches.' Flint snorted. 'Right now a whole lot of frightened folk wouldn't thank you for doing that, Dan.'

'I guess not,' Dan conceded, and asked, 'Is there a point to this conversation, Arthur?'

'Did Sam Burns buy the south valley?'

Dan Straker shook his head.

'Then, I reckon, that there's a point to this conversation, Dan.'

Cyrus Hanley had intended hanging out in Mexico for a spell longer than his impetuous act of bucking Jack Galt allowed him to. Now, riding with no particular direction in mind and constantly switching trails to try and throw the Galt gang off his scent, he was a man living on his nerves. Being pursued by Galt was not his only worry. He was riding through country where the next turn in the trail could bring him face to face with a lawman or a bounty hunter with a pocket stuffed with dodgers. His head was not worth much, fifty dollars maybe. Most bounty hunters would not take the trouble, but if times were hard and cash was short, a man might figure that fifty dollars was better than no dollars at all. A couple of times he had felt eyes on him. Imagination? Indians, maybe? Just another danger in a land full of threat and menace, where a man lived his life a second at a time.

Of all the threats to his hide, there was no doubt that Jack Galt catching him up was the one that haunted him every minute, including the few he slept. His quandary and frustration was that, though haste was of the essence, caution was necessary. Often, a man caught between, made the kind of mistakes that were his undoing.

*

With mounting disbelief, Dan Straker listened to the scheme Flint and his partners had hatched. Concluding, the storekeeper asked eagerly, 'What do you say, Dan?'

'I think it's a loco idea,' Straker stated bluntly. 'A man might as well put a gun to his own head as go up against Jack Galt, Arthur.'

'Even for two thousand dollars?' Flint said, quietly. Temptation dangled, he went on quickly, 'Two thousand could divert that mountain stream, pay your debts, Dan.' Straker wavering, Flint sweetened his temptation. 'And it would give Mary a respite.'

'If there's any merit in this crazy scheme, that's it!' Straker growled.

Flint had more cards to play.

'If Galt comes calling, Dan, who's to say that his spite will end in town. There's Mary, and you know how Jack Galt treats women.'

The lurid stories of Galt's excesses in the years since the end of the Civil War often had Dan Straker regretting having saved the Georgian's life.

'Having saved Galt's life, he'll be beholden, Dan. If he'll listen to anyone, it'll be you.'

Straker said sombrely, 'And if he doesn't listen, Arthur?'

The storekeeper unequivocally stated, 'Then I guess that two thousand dollars is going to be harder to earn, Dan.'

Dan Straker's face curled sourly. 'Blood money!'

'Call it bounty,' Arthur Flint suggested.

'No difference.'

Flint said, 'Talk it over with Mary. Let me know what you've decided. But remember, time is short. Ben Galt had back-up in town. By now he's well on his way to where Galt is holed up.' Grimly, the storekeeper finished, 'If he's not already there.'

Straker cautioned, 'With the law from almost every state and territory on Jack Galt's tail, he'll move around a lot. This close to the border, he's probably in Mexico. Finding a needle in a haystack takes time, Arthur.'

Suspecting that Dan was making his task sound more difficult to up the ante, Flint argued, 'There's only a couple of trails up out of Mexico that's headed our way, Dan.'

'Men like Jack Galt don't use the regular trails, Arthur. They use Indian trails. Old prospector trails. Routes handed on from outlaw to outlaw . . . like I said, a needle in a haystack. Finding Galt would need a great dollop of luck. I might never find him, leastways not in time.'

'But you'll try, won't you?'

An outright refusal now would force Flint to play his last card. Blackmail. Dan Straker had taken pains to bury Josh Lawson and would not want him resurrected. Him and his partners had talked about saving their money and going straight for blackmail, but feared Straker's reaction should their underhandedness backfire.

Dan sifted Flint's question for nuance, and decided that it was more a threat than a question. He was not, nor never had been a man who took kindly to threats.

'I'll talk to Mary.' The storekeeper was riding away when Dan said, 'I'm telling you, and you tell your friends, Arthur. Never did like blackmailers. Try it, and I'll kill you all.'

Flint protested, but his protestation waned under Straker's icy stare. In the final seconds of their meeting the amiable Dan Straker had given way to the hidden Josh Lawson. The storekeeper rode away, sweat trickling down his spine, thankful that he was still breathing.

CHAPTER EIGHT

At dinner that evening, Mary Straker keenly observed her husband's lack of appetite. 'I know that meat pie isn't exactly the finest grub in the county, Dan,' she said, lightly, 'but it isn't as bad as you're making out, poking at it the way you have been.'

Shaken out of his reverie, Dan enthused, 'The meat pie's fine, Mary. You could make my old boots tasty.'

Mary scolded him, 'Tell me what's worrying you, Dan.'

His eyes widened. 'Worrying me, Mary? Nothing's worrying me.'

'You're lying to me, Dan,' she stated bluntly. 'And when a man starts lying, he puts his head in a noose that will finally choke him!'

Straker immediately dropped his charade of innocence – there was no fooling Mary. After his meeting with Arthur Flint, Dan had pondered until his head hurt. He had come up with a hundred spurious reasons to take the store-keeper's bounty, all of which were built on sand. The fact was, there was no excuse for taking money to kill another man, even one as scurrilous as Jack Galt. Nevertheless, Dan had dreams of seeing Mary glow again like she used to in the early morning after sleep, and in the evening when the day's work was done, a different kind of glow then, but both equally enchanting and beguiling.

And he had visions of lush earth and fields of proud crops.

Even if he took Flint's blood money, he might not be around to see any of these things. He was fast with a gun, but faster than Jack Galt? Debatable. Galt would have one card in the deck that he would not have, and that was his honed and ruthless killer's instinct. Whereas he had killed men in self-protection, or in his duty as a lawman, Jack Galt killed men simply for the pleasure it gave him. Simply stated, Straker would give Galt a fair chance, but Galt would kill him in whatever way he could. If a bullet in the back would suffice, then Jack Galt would have no qualms about doing just that.

'What's fretting you so, Dan?' He cursed himself for not having shucked his dour mood before sitting to table. Mary's burdens were heavy enough without him adding to them. 'Did you meet up with Arthur Flint?'

Straker's downcast head shot up.

'He dropped by looking for you shortly after you left for Sam Burns' place. Followed on. All this moody pondering is to do with him, isn't it?'

Dan smiled. 'I'm married to a shrewd woman. You don't let a man keep his secrets for long, Mary.'

There was nothing for it but to tell Mary about his meeting with Flint. As always, she heard Dan out before giving her opinion. Her view was uncompromisingly stark.

'Killing a man for profit isn't right, Dan. Plain and simple.'

'All our problems would fly out the window,' Straker argued.

'Dan,' she said, 'I've loved you for your gentleness and goodness. It's what marked you out as a man in a country that has too many men ready to resort to the use of a gun. Change that, and I'm not sure I could love you as much, if at all.'

'I used a gun plenty in Quido, Mary,' he pointed out.

'Different,' she countered. 'This time, if you take Arthur Flint's money, you won't be wearing a marshal's badge when you'll kill Jack Galt.' Her gaze was rock-steady. 'That is, Dan, *if* you kill Jack Galt.' She stood up and went to look out the window, her back to him. 'That's as plainly as I know how to put it, Dan. After that the choice is yours.'

He got up, took her in his arms, and hugged her

like he'd never hugged her before. 'I knew when I married you that you were a good woman, Mary Duff. But until this moment, I didn't fully realize how good you really are.'

He kissed her with a passion that left her breathless.

'Oh, Dan Straker,' she playfully scolded him, 'stop your philandering right this second. You've got to eat that meat pie before it'll drop right through your belly, it'll be so darn heavy.'

Leading her to the bedroom, Dan said, 'Meat pie, be damned!'

It was midway through a sleepless night for Dan, when Mary woke.

'What if I tried to persuade Galt to—'

'Persuade?'

'Talk to him.'

'Talk to Jack Galt?' Mary scoffed.

'Galt's beholden, Mary.'

'Beholden? How?'

'I saved his life.'

'You saved Jack Galt's life?' Mary yelped, shooting straight up in bed. 'That wasn't the brightest thing you ever did.' A worried frown furrowed her brow. 'Dan, Galt's got a canker of badness in him that's pure evil.'

Dan joked, 'If it came to it, I'm a good runner, Mary.'

Soberly, Mary reminded him, 'You can't run with a bullet in your head, Dan.'

Quietly, in a voice as still as the night, Dan Straker told his wife, 'Flint knows who I am, Mary.'

Mary asked, in a voice as hushed as Dan's, 'How?'

'Ned Billings showed up in town today, right in the middle of the commotion, saw me and grabbed his chance to earn some easy money by telling Flint and his business cronies about Josh Lawson. I have no doubt that if I don't accept Flint's proposition my past will become tomorrow's news.'

Mary sat up in bed. 'You think Arthur would—'

'I don't know, but desperate needs make for desperate deeds, Mary. Ben Galt's death has put Eagle Junction in line for Jack Galt's revenge. Folk are afraid, and fear makes men do things that they normally would not even consider doing.'

His voice dropped to the merest whisper.

'I guess when it comes down to it, all this talk is nothing more than smoke in a bottle, honey.' Sombrely, he said, 'I don't have a choice. Word will get out somehow, always does. Billings for one will spread it. And when that happens, it would be best to have enough to make a new start.'

Mary Straker, having fought against admitting as much to herself, now conceded the inevitabilty of Dan's involvement in the dangerous task of coming face to face with Jack Galt.

The next morning, at first light, Dan Straker was hammering on Arthur Flint's door. As he rode into town he noticed edgy men on the hotel roof and in the church tower, and from the shadows along Main he heard the click of a gun being readied as he approached, until a voice called out:

'Hello, Dan. Up before the crows, ain't you.'

The man not revealing himself, Dan simply tipped his hat and continued on to Flint's house at the far end of Main.

When he answered the hammering on his door the storekeeper was grumpy, but on seeing Dan his eyes flashed with hope. 'You've decided to take me up on my proposition, Dan?'

'I reckon that there was never a chance that I couldn't. But I'll try and persuade Galt first.'

'Persuade?'

Flint shook his head doubtfully.

'That's what I'll try to do, Arthur.'

'And if Galt won't listen?'

'Then, I'll have to kill him, won't I. Or,' Dan shrugged, 'at least try.'

'Is Mary OK with this, Dan? She could end up a widder woman.'

'Handling a rattler like Jack Galt always brings that risk,' Dan stated. 'And it's payment up front.'

'Up front?' the storekeeper yelped.

'If I don't come back, Mary will need the money to make it back home and for her widowhood. Two thousand clear, and all slates wiped clean.'

'I don't know, Dan . . . .'

'Fine by me.'

Dan Straker strode to the door, confident that he had Flint over a barrel. He had.

'OK,' Flint said sourly. 'The bank. In an hour.'

Dan Straker had performed many difficult and heart-breaking tasks in his life, but the hardest task he had ever had to endure was riding away from Mary that day. He had overcome her protestations about moving into town to stay at the Flint house during his absence. Holding Mary to him he told her, 'Whatever happens, I want you to know that the happiest years of my life have been the ones I've spent with you. And I aim to have lots more.'

Though Mary Straker knew the chances were that she would be a widow, she hid her fear and resolutely made plans for her man's return. Because the only alternative was to pitch headlong into grief and insanity.

'Are we going to sit 'round this shithole for ever, Jack?' Raul Sanchez questioned.

Jack Galt, his hands exploring under a whore's petticoat, reacted angrily to the Mexican's criticism-laced question. 'We go when I say we go,' the gang leader snarled.

A man of insatiable passions, the whore had pleased Jack Galt for longer than any woman had. Her tricks, many and varied had ensnared Galt, and the gang knew that they would have to wait, irrespective of how much they protested, until their leader's libido was satisfied. It might be another hour, another day, week or month. It was simply the way of things.

Sanchez said, 'The boys and me want to catch up with that Hanley coyote, Jack, before he vanishes.'

It was a lame reason. Galt could dally for a year and still find Hanley. It might take a while longer, but find him he would.

'And,' Sanchez added, when there was no benefit accruing from his first ploy, 'there's the little matter of revenging Ben's killing.'

'Jack, baby,' the whore cooed as Galt lost interest in her.

'Ah!' the gang leader threw the woman to the floor. 'I've had enough of you.' Now afraid of Galt's sudden anger, the whore crept away. He called to the barkeep. 'Whiskey, my friend. Lots of whiskey.' He slapped his hand on the table. 'Tonight,' he told his men, 'we get drunk like we've never been drunk before. Then,' his eyes narrowed to slits, 'tomorrow we ride to revenge Ben's murder!'

CHAPTER NINE

Dan Straker looked out across the scorched land. Heat rose off the desert floor in great shimmering waves, and the sun burned mercilessly on his shoulders and back. The cabin, in a place that made no sense, was a welcome sight. He closed his eyes, fearing that when he opened them again, the cabin would have vanished, a figment of his over-wrought mind, but it was still there. So were the horses in the corral behind the cabin. From the ridge, looking into the sun, they looked spritely enough, but up close they might turn out to be as mangy as his own mount whose legs were buckling.

He was three days into his search. He had asked about Jack Galt's whereabouts along the way. Some folk had gone dumb on hearing the Georgian's name; others had gone ashen-faced, and he was no nearer to finding out where the outlaw was. Understandably, no one wanted to earn Galt's wrath.

'Have ya got a hole in yer head, mister,' one old-timer had asked him. 'You must wanna be dead real bad, goin' after Jack Galt.' The old man's rheumy eyes had searched Straker's chest for a star, and finding none, he had assumed that Dan was a bounty hunter. 'Ain't 'nuff money been made for a man to tangle with Galt,' he opined.

As he continued his search, scouring trail after trail, the old-timer's view proved to be a common one. But Dan knew that it would be luck rather than strategy which would bring him face-to-face with Jack Galt. He could search as many trails again, but there would always be one more and, he suspected, Galt would know them all.

Galt had probably been in Mexico, and was likely on the move by now. All he could do was search the most direct routes to Eagle Junction, in the hope that Galt's ire would have him take the direct route. But the outlaw might also take an old Indian or prospector's trail, which he would know nothing of.

Straker was, he knew, looking for that needle he talked about in a mighty big haystack.

Dan let his jaded horse find its own way down the rocky path from the ridge, ready to leap from the saddle should the beast's legs give out. He had walked the horse for long spells, but it had made little difference – the mare was finished. The softer soil of the desert floor sapped the last of the horse's energy, and she barely made it to the cabin yard before keeling over. Her eyes rolled and the breath rattled in her throat. Dan shot the suffering beast between the eyes.

'Drop the gun, mister.'

Dan, on hearing a bullet slot into the breach of the rifle behind him, did not argue.

'Hands in the air.'

Dan obeyed.

'Now, turn slowly,' the woman instructed, and added, 'Very slowly, mister. So much as a twitch and I'll blast you.'

'I believe you, ma'am,' Dan said. And he did.

He turned as he had been told to, and his jaw dropped on seeing the girl holding the gun on him, thirteen at most he reckoned.

'Mighty big gun for a little lady,' he commented.

'I ain't too little to plug you, mister.'

'Can you shoot that thing?' Dan drawled.

The bullet that grazed his right toecap answered his question, and the second bullet that fanned his left cheek left no doubt at all. Dancing back, Dan said, 'I'm convinced.'

'Emily . . . .'

Dan's glance went to the woman on crutches in the cabin door, her face haggard beyond her years, and the ninety-year-old hump to her shoulders weighed her down. There had been fear in her voice, and there was fear now in her eyes on seeing the dishevelled man in the yard. Strangers, in a land where danger and death were never far away, could be a blessing if it was trade or companionship they were seeking. Or a curse if it was trouble they had in mind.

'It's OK, Ma,' Emily called back. 'I got him covered.'

'What d'ya want here, mister?' the woman asked, in a tone of voice that held the timbre of a no-nonsense woman.

'A horse, ma'am,' Dan replied. 'As you can see, mine's just given up the ghost.'

'A horse, huh?'

'Yes, ma'am.'

'Got money?'

'Some. Not much. But, from what I've seen of your nags, I won't need much.'

The woman laughed. 'A lippy sort, ain't ya.'

'Stating it as I see it, ma'am,' Dan said. 'That's my way.'

'It's a good way, too,' she said. 'Walk this way, till I see ya proper. My eyes ain't what they used to be, looking all the time into this damn sun.'

'Yes, ma'am.'

'Keep that shooter steady on him, Emily,' the woman said. 'Any tricks, you plug him. And make it count.'

Dan began to walk towards the cabin, Emily pacing him, Winchester primed.

'That's far 'nuff, mister,' the girl warned Straker, as he drew near the cabin porch. 'You can do your talkin' from where you stand.'

Dan grinned at the woman. 'A real spark of a gal

you've got there, ma'am.'

'Horse, ya say?' the woman said. She shook her head and laughed. 'Mosta my nags are 'bout as lively as the one you've just shot.' She hobbled to the side of the porch and pointed a crutch to the corral. 'That black's 'bout the best, and Lord knows he ain't no great shakes. Kinda slack-sided. Ain't much feed round here. He'll tire fast.'

'You're an honest woman,' Dan complimented.

'No, I ain't. But I reckon you're a man who knows horseflesh, so there'd be no point in me tryin' to fool ya.' She laughed. 'Would if I could though.'

Dan walked to the corral to look the black over.

'Keep that Winchester on him, Emily,' the woman warned. 'Seems OK, but he's not the first wolf in sheep's clothin' that's come a-callin'.'

'I've got ev'ry inch of him covered good and proper, Ma.'

'That's my girl.'

Straker said, 'Can't say that I feel comfortable doing business with a gun at my back, ma'am. I'm not aiming to cause you or the girl any grief.'

The woman considered Dan's remarks for a moment, and then called the girl off. 'Let the man be, honey.'

'You sure 'bout that, Ma?'

'Yeah. I figure we've got a good one here, daughter. There's honesty in his gait.'

'If you say so, Ma,' Emily said, doubtfully.

The woman said, 'You look all you want, mister. Then come inside the house to parley when you're ready to.'

Dan tipped his hat. 'Obliged, ma'am.'

'Elinora's the name, if you have a mind to use it – Elinora Clancy from County Kerry, that would be.'

Dan continued on to the corral. After a cursory examination of the horses, Elinora's opinion was borne out. The black, though not in the best of trim, was his only hope. The others had but a two-spit journey in them. He returned to the house. Elinora was seated in a cane chair, her face curled in pain. This close, the smell of a rotting leg was overpowering. Elinora Clancy, quick to spot the twitch of Straker's nostrils, said:

'I know. Sniffin' round me ain't none too pleasant.' She pointed to her right leg which curved just above the ankle. 'Broke it a coupla days 'go. Darn fool thing to do way out here. Emily, bless her heart, did her best with splintin' it.'

Dan stated the obvious, 'It needs doctoring pretty bad.'

'Ain't no sawbones, 'ceptin you can travel twenty miles to Deepsville, or Doc Fanshaw drops by.'

'Fanshaw? Remember seeing his wagon in Eagle Junction last fall.' Dan was sceptical. 'That leg of yours needs a proper medico, Elinora.'

'Fanshaw is a proper sawbones,' Elinora assured Dan. 'Got a fancy piece o' paper an' all to prove it.'

Dan's scepticism remained. 'Runs a medicine show 'cause he got tired o' sittin' in an office all the time. Horace Fanshaw is a man with a sense of adventure.'

If only Mary were here, Dan thought, she'd have that leg cleaned and splinted in no time at all. But he'd learned a fair share of doctoring himself in the war, and from necessity he'd set many a broken limb.

'If you want,' he said. 'I can look-see.'

The woman snorted. 'Think mebbe it's too late?'

'Can't say. I'm not a doctor, but,' he stated honestly, 'in this heat it can't be in the best shape.'

'Can you really do somethin', mister?' Emily asked, her blue eyes filling with tears. 'Ma's been in real bad pain.'

'You go outside, honey,' Elinora said, 'let me and the gent talk. Keep a hawk eye out for any strangers, ya hear.'

'You bet, Ma.'

Reluctantly, Emily left.

'I'll get a fire going,' Dan said. 'Boil some water.'

Elinora grabbed his arm. 'Don't waste your time, mister. The poison's well into me by now. I can feel its venom takin' hold.'

'You can't be sure of that, Elinora.'

'I'm sure,' she snapped impatiently. 'I've been prayin', and I figure the Lord's answered.' Her feverish gaze settled on Straker, refusing to let his eyes escape. 'Emily's well-bein' is all that matters now. I sense that you're a good man. Take her under your wing, mister.'

Dan was stunned. 'I can't do that, Elinora.'

'You got that married look. You married?'

'Yes.'

'Kids?'

'No. Mary can't have kids.'

'Then Emily can be your daughter.'

'Hasn't she got a father?' Dan desperately questioned.

'Feedin' worms out back. Only his liver won't be much good to them with all the moonshine it soaked up.' Angrily, she said, 'Don't look 'way. You gotta name?'

'Dan Straker.'

'Well, Dan, will ya help Emily to see womanhood? 'Nother coupla days, a week maybe, and she'll be orphaned. There's no hope for her here. She'll die slowly.'

'Let me see that leg of yours.'

'Look all you want. It won't matter none.'

Dan undid the makeshift splint and filthy dressing. Revealed, the injury made his stomach heave.

'Told ya so,' Elinora said. Then, pleading, 'At least see Emily safely to Deepsville, Dan, I'm beggin' ya. Find a family that will take her in.'

Dan stalked to the window, his mind fighting with his heart. However, it did not take long for him to arrive at a decision; the only decision a decent man could reach. He turned from the window. 'Deepsville it'll be, Elinora.'

'You'll do your best to see that Emily is in safe keeping, won't you, Dan?'

'That I will.'

Elinora Clancy's relief was palpable. 'Thank you, Jesus,' she prayed. She wiped away her tears as soon as they flowed. 'We've got to come up with a plausible reason for Emily goin' to Deepsville with you. Got any ideas, Dan?'

'Guess I'll tell her that she's going to fetch the doc, and show him the way back here.'

'That's a fine reason. I'll call her in here right now. Emily,' she hollered.

The girl hurried inside, suspicious eyes on Straker, rifle again at the ready.

'Put the rifle away, honey,' Elinora said. 'Come sit by me.' Elinora hugged her, her saddened eyes on Dan. 'Mr Straker here is goin' to do us a big favour, Emily. He's goin' to take you to Deepsville to fetch the doc to see to this busted leg o' mine.'

'You are, mister?' Emily enthused, her eyes glowing with hope.

'Sure am, Emily,' Dan assured her.

'Then you show the sawbones the way back here, 'cause Mr Straker's got other chores that need doin', honey. Can you do that for me?'

'Sure I can, Ma.'

'That's my treasure, Dan,' Elinora Clancy said.

'You take good care of her. I'll be waitin' right here for her return.'

Straker promised, 'I'll see that Emily's safe and well, Elinora.'

Elinora Clancy lay back in her chair, spent. 'That pleases me, Dan,' she said. A great burden lifted, her eyes wearily closed. 'Pleases me greatly, indeed.'

Emily prepared a meagre meal before they set off for Deepsville. Though Dan could see that her heart was broken, Elinora Clancy maintained her smile and bonhomie until Dan and Emily put distance between them. Then she closed the cabin door, and began her grim wait for death to take her.

CHAPTER TEN

Coming out of the thoughtful mood she had slipped into, Emily asked Straker, 'Ma's goin' to be all right ain't she, Mr Straker?'

'Of course she is, Emily,' he lied, and worried about how betrayed she would feel when he would have to tell her the truth. 'We'll be back with a doctor before you know it.'

Emily Clancy enthused, 'We'd best quicken our pace, Mr Straker.'

'Easy.' Dan grabbed her pony's reins. 'We can't push these nags too far, Emily. We don't want them folding under us, now do we?'

'Heck, no.'

'Then follow my lead, nice and slow.'

Emily grinned. 'Sure thing, Mr Straker. Glad I didn't plug ya right off when I set eyes on ya.'

Dan grinned. 'Me, too.'

' 'Cause, you didn't look like no gent in them dusty duds you're in.'

'Well,' Dan promised, 'next time I'll come calling, I'll be sure to pretty myself up.'

With childish honesty, Emily Clancy announced, 'That'd sure be smart, Mr Straker, 'cause you're kinda handsome, and cleaned up some you'd be real handsome.'

'Why, thank you, Emily. But don't you go swelling my head and make it so heavy that I'll be tumbling off this nag.'

Emily laughed skittishly. 'Gee, Mr Straker, that's silly. No one's head could swell that darn much.'

They rode on through the long afternoon in companionable silence, until they came to a creek that hadn't much more than a mouthful of water in it, but lots of welcome shade to rest under.

'We ain't stoppin', are we?' Emily challenged Dan. 'We've got to keep goin' to Deepsville.'

Dan reasoned, 'If our horses buckle, it's likely that we'll never make it to Deepsville. We'll rest here tonight, and head out again at first light.'

'But ma is hurtin' real bad,' she protested.

'First light, Emily,' Dan insisted.

Some age-old instinct twanged Straker's nerves. 'You wait here, Emily,' he said, 'while I check out the creek.'

'What's to check out. It's just a creek.'

'Might be rattlers,' he said.

Emily shivered. 'Rattlers. I hate rattlers.'

'Then it's best if I make sure there aren't any lurking. Makes sense, doesn't it?'

'I guess.'

Dan said, 'Why don't you slide into those trees, huh. Out of the sun.'

'It ain't that warm.'

'Still . . .' Dan gently nudged her horse into the trees. A blue ribbon tying Emily's blond hair snagged on a bush and she winced. Dan urged her to be quiet while he checked out the creek. 'Rattlers have really good hearing.'

Emily was doubtful on this point. Dan did not know either way, but it was a plausible enough story, he reckoned. He figured that it was a tale that he could not be challenged on, because no one knew if rattlers were as deaf as stones or had needle-sharp hearing, or even had ears.

Dan approached the creek, every nerve alert, his hand hovering over his .45. The creek was quiet – too quiet, maybe. The only sound disturbing the Boothill stillness was the trickle of water negotiating the stony bed of the creek, and that was something that a lurker could not stop. But he could scare away birds and creatures who were sensitive to danger.

Dan rode to the edge of the creek, dismounted, and replenished his canteen. The creek water could be sour and possibly gut-infecting, but it was all the water there was on offer so he'd have to risk its dangers.

He began to whistle tunelessly, because he was tone deaf. He hoped that his ear-hurting whistle would serve two purposes, one, that any lurker would take it that he was unaware of his presence and, two, that it would settle his own nerves. But all it did was make his mouth and throat drier than it already was.

After a couple of minutes Dan heard what he was expecting, the hammer of a six gun being thumbed back.

CHAPTER ELEVEN

'Say who you are and what you're up to, mister,' a croaky voice, sandy dry from thirst, demanded.

'Easy on that trigger, mister,' Dan said, and complied. 'The name's Dan Straker. I'm escorting a kid to Deepsville.'

'A kid?' the man asked suspiciously. 'Don't see no kid.'

'Back in the trees a bit. Reckoned I'd check out the creek before bringing her on further.'

'Wise,' was the gun-toter's opinion. Seconds ticked by before the man said, 'Turn real slow.'

'I'm getting mighty teed off with all this repetition,' Dan mumbled.

'How's that?'

'This is the second time today that someone's got the drop on me.'

'Who else, 'sides me?'

'The kid.'

The man chuckled. 'The kid?'

'A real she-cat,' Dan said.

'That a fact,' the gun-toter snorted.

'Sure is, mister.'

Dan grinned on hearing the Winchester's breach being readied. 'Toss your gun in the creek,' Emily ordered Dan's tormentor.

'I'd do it, mister,' Dan advised the man. 'That kid's got a short fuse.'

'Right into the middle, too,' Emily ordered the gun-toter.

'What if I shoot this fella?' the man speculated.

'Then I blast you,' Emily announced matter-of-factly, 'and be done with it.'

A six gun was tossed over Dan's shoulder into the middle of the creek.

Emily said, 'Frisk him, Dan. Might have a second gun or a knife. Looks a shifty *hombre* to me, and that's a fact.'

Dan swung about to face a bemused Cyrus Hanley. 'Kind of belittling for a kid to get the drop on you, isn't it. I know the feeling.'

Dan slid his hands over Hanley, who snarled, 'Like me? Or are you just efficient, mister?'

Dan Straker grinned. 'I've seen prettier coyotes, fella.'

'In the dark I'm real handsome,' Hanley flung back.

'What're you two gabbin' 'bout?' Emily wanted to know.

'Just talk, Emily,' Dan said. He settled his gaze on Hanley, and slammed a fist in his face. Hanley shot backwards and collided with a tree. His back arched in pain. 'Don't like sneakers,' Dan grated. 'Now, it's my turn to ask you who you are, and what you're doing here?'

Angry as a polecat, but helpless under the threat of Emily Clancy's Winchester, the outlaw growled, 'Monicker's Cyrus Hanley. Riding through.'

'Shoot him, Emily,' Straker ordered.

'Hold it!'

'Talk,' Dan ordered Hanley.

The outlaw stalled. 'How do I know that you're not one of Jack Galt's men?'

Dan scoffed. 'Towing a kid?'

'Yeah,' Hanley conceded. 'Don't make sense.'

'Jack Galt, huh?' Dan said, in as casual a tone as he could manage with his heart racing the way it was. Had he stumbled on a line to Galt? 'You're running from Galt?'

'I'm runnin',' Hanley confirmed.

'Strange world, isn't it?'

'Huh?'

'You running – me looking.'

'For Galt?' Cyrus Hanley exclaimed. He shook his head fit to come off his shoulders. 'No one sane looks for Jack Galt, fella. Might as well go lookin' for the Grim Reaper. Same thing.' Then, curiosity outweighing apprehension, because uninvited questions in the West could bring a swift and painful reaction, the outlaw enquired, 'Why're you lookin'?'

'It's a long story.' Hanley's gaze went Emily's way. 'But first I'm headed to Deepsville to bring back a doc for Emily's sick ma.'

'How come you've got the time to be a Good Samaritan, when you're on Galt's trail?'

Straker ignored the question, and instead asked a question: 'Know where Galt is right now?'

'Mebbe.' Cyrus Hanley had a trading chip, and he knew it. 'Tell the kid to sheath the rifle.'

Dan nodded to Emily.

'Don't know, Mr Straker,' Emily said. 'Like I said, looks kinda shifty to me.'

'He hasn't got a gun, Emily,' Dan said. 'I have.'

Emily holstered the Winchester, grumbling, 'Sure hope this ain't a mistake, Dan.'

It was the first time Emily had called him by his christian name, and the way she said it had a real cosy ring to it. Instantly conscious of her impudence, Emily apologized, 'Gee, I'm real sorry, Mr Straker. Kinda slipped out beknown to me.'

'Dan will do just fine, Emily,' Straker reassured the girl. 'Just fine.'

'That so, Dan?' Emily yelped. Then cooed, 'Dan,' testing the sound of his name.

Dan Straker's attention returned to Cyrus Hanley. 'Cards on the table?'

'Suits me just fine.'

'Galt's brother, Ben, caught lead in a town called Eagle Junction.'

'I know.'

'You do?'

'Ben Galt had a back-up – a fool. He came back to tell Jack Galt about Ben. Galt staked him out for wild dogs to devour.' Emily paled. Dan drew Hanley out of Emily's hearing. 'I shot him to rid him of his misery.'

'I bet that didn't endear you to Jack Galt.'

'No, sir,' Hanley confirmed.

'How come Galt didn't kill you there and then?'

Hanley speculated, 'Guess he liked the idea of huntin' me down. Galt's mad as hell. Sure wouldn't like to be living in Eagle Junction, with him on the way.' With genuine interest, the outlaw asked, 'Why're you lookin' for Jack Galt, mister?'

'To try and persuade him not to take revenge on Eagle Junction for his brother's killing.'

Cyrus Hanley scoffed, 'Stop Jack Galt doin' what he plans? You're dreamin' while you're wide 'wake, fella!' Then, he enquired, 'Why would stoppin' Galt fall to you?'

'None of your damn business,' Dan snapped.

'It is if you want my help in finding Galt.'

Another trading chip. Damn!

'The town is paying me to talk to Galt.'

'Talk? This yarn gets crazier all the time.' Bemused and bewildered, Cyrus Hanley checked, 'Let me get this straight. You figure that jawin' with Jack Galt will make him change his mind 'bout revengin' his brother Ben's killin'? Craziest thing I ever heard.'

Stated so succinctly, for the first time Dan Straker realized how crazy his scheme was. Lamely, he said, 'It's a long shot I know—'

'Long shot?' Hanley derided. 'It's way over the moon and some more.' Bluntly, he stated, 'You're a fool. Galt'll rip your guts out and feed them to the buzzards, Straker.'

'Talking about foolishness,' Dan said, 'it wasn't too clever of you to get on the wrong side of Jack Galt. How come you did?'

'Well,' Hanley began, 'I ain't exactly covered myself in glory these past coupla years, lived pretty much to keep my own hide intact.' His mouth twisted in a grimace of disgust. 'But what Jack Galt did to Ike Cramer, the fella who brought him word of his brother's death, churned my innards a mite too much.' He sighed. 'Broke the first and only outlaw rule. I let my heart rule my head.' Cyrus Hanley's shoulders slumped as if someone had just placed the world on them. 'Should have minded my own damn business, o' course, like I always have. Gone and signed my own death warrant now.' He shook his head. 'No matter what hole I hide in, Galt'll find me.'

'Know the trail up from Mexico that Galt is likely to ride?' Straker asked.

'Lots o' trails, Straker.'

'So I've been finding out,' Dan groaned.

'If you take my advice, you'll forget 'bout findin' Galt. Keep ridin', too. You don't wanna be in Eagle

Junction when the Galt gang rides in.'

'My wife is in Eagle Junction.'

'Then get back there fast and get her out,' Hanley advised.

'You said you'd help me find Galt,' Straker challenged.

Hanley took his hat off and wiped his brow. 'Guess all this sun gives a man a fool's tongue. I'm headin' outa this country as fast as I can. So I'll just get my gun from the creek and hightail it.'

'Maybe,' Dan began slowly, 'your story is a whole lot of bull, Hanley.' The outlaw paused in mid-stride. Dan continued with his speculation, 'Maybe you're one of the Galt gang . . .' Hanley drew his trailing leg level with the other and stood stock-still. 'You could be riding right to Galt to tell him about me. And . . . .'

Cyrus Hanley turned slowly.

'Maybe I should kill you right here and now.'

CHAPTER TWELVE

After a lengthy perusal of Dan Straker, Cyrus Hanley opined, 'I reckon that you're not the cold-blooded kind o' killer it would take to pull that trigger for no good reason other than what you think might be, mister.'

'What if you're wrong?' Straker bluffed.

Growing in confidence, Hanley said, 'If I was, we wouldn't be gabbin'. I'd be dead.'

Dan holstered his .45.

Cyrus Hanley retrieved his pistol from the creek and got in the saddle. 'What I told you was no yarn,' he told Dan. He rode off, but drew rein and swung about. 'Ya know, maybe travellin' t'gether, we'd stand a better chance if we cross trails with the Galt outfit.'

'Two guns are always better than one,' Dan said.

'Three guns,' Emily Clancy corrected.

Cyrus Hanley dismounted. 'You got grub?'

'Not much.'

'Me neither.'

Dan held out his hand. Hanley shook hands with a firm grasp. 'Let's see what we can rustle up 'tween us, Dan. I'll get some kindlin' to get a fire goin'.'

Dan watched the outlaw as he gathered a bundle of kindling, his thoughts alternating between dark and kindly. Could Cyrus Hanley's sudden change of heart be down to something other than a desire for friendship and common purpose? Could he be a Galt man, leading him and Emily into a trap? Or, if his story about being on the run from Jack Galt was true, might he be figuring on trading him and Emily to Galt in return for his own safety?

Huddled around the campfire from the chill of the desert night, Dan asked, 'What got you on to the owlhoot trail, Cyrus?'

'Robbed a bank that was trying to rob me.' He told Dan about the bank's underhanded shenanigans. 'Foreclosed when there was no good reason to. Stole my farm right from under me to sell on the cheap to a rich crony.'

He scratched his head.

'Got in a coupla fights.' He laughed. 'One time, shot the hat clean off a marshal's head. No big deal, not if a goodly patch of the lawman's hair wasn't in his hat.'

Relaxed, his guard down, Dan said, 'That wouldn't be Patch Johnson, would it?'

'You know Johnson?'

Dan knew that he had blundered.

'Oh, in passing,' Dan said, hoping that his casual dismissal of the acquaintance would satisfy the outlaw's curiosity and stop him pondering as he now was. A lot of water had flowed downstream since he had been the badge-toter in Quido, and he had changed some. However, a man with his curiosity piqued might have his memory jogged.

Dan stretched and yawned. 'Guess I'll turn in.'

'Kinda early,' Hanley said in a preoccupied drawl, his eyes following Straker as he made a big deal of laying out his blankets.

'Been a long day.'

Straker's tone discouraged further conversation. 'Yeah.'

It looked like the outlaw had let go of the bone he had been chewing on, but he was far from being tired enough to sleep. That meant he'd have lots of thinking time. Dan figured that his hurry to get into his blankets, instead of engaging Hanley in conversation to try and divert his mind away from thinking about him, might have been his second blunder.

It was.

The fire had burned to embers when Hanley asked, 'Ever been to Quido, Dan?'

CHAPTER THIRTEEN

'Quido?' Straker asked casually, maybe too casually. 'Never heard of it.' He added lightly, 'Sounds Canadian to me. Never been to Canada. 'Night.'

Dan lay awake long after Hanley's snores filled the creek, his thoughts first of Mary and all the golden years that would go a-begging if his desperate attempt to secure their future went fatally awry. His second thoughts were of Elinora Clancy, another good woman, wasted away by the harsh and cruel land they lived in.

If he survived his ordeal, Dan wondered if he should use Flint's bounty to quit and seek out new pastures, or maybe even throw in his lot with Sam and Tommy Duff, if Tommy had begun to see that the war had rights and wrongs on both sides. For a lot of Southerners the adage that time heals did not apply, and displays of Yankee triumphalism reopened old wounds for further festering. The healing of division, often rabid and cancerous, particularly post-Civil War, would be a fraught passage needing men of goodwill on both sides to come to the fore and face down the bigots who would have the carnage revisited. Someone had to take the first step, and maybe it was now time to stand toe to toe with Tommy Duff and talk man to man, rather than regurgitating old arguments that had lost their relevance in the new United States of America.

Breakfast over, if that's what coffee made with sour water could be called, Dan outlined his plans much to Cyrus Hanley's discomfiture.

'Goin' to Deepsville will eat up time,' Hanley argued, and cautioned, 'Time that Jack Galt might use to make tracks to Eagle Junction.'

'I promised Emily's ma that I'd get her there.'

'Always keep your promises, do ya?' the outlaw groused.

'I sure try,' Dan answered, honestly. 'Anyway, we can't take a kid along to meet Galt. A girl, at that.'

'Guess you gotta point,' Hanley conceded. 'I wouldn't put an old crone in Jack Galt's way. That honcho's got an appetite for women that ain't natural.' He gazed thoughtfully at Emily. 'Hand him a fine young thing like Emily, and Galt might forgive a man anything.' Dan Straker's eyes shot Hanley's way. 'The young'r, the better Galt likes 'em.'

The outlaw climbed into the saddle.

'Let's move out. Keep those eyes peeled for

'Paches, as well as any other critter we might cross paths with. Indians are mostly tame, but hungry. Nothing like hunger to rile a man, when the land of his ancestors ain't his no more.'

Surprised, Straker said, 'You sound like an—' Dan chewed off his words. A lot of men took deep offence at what he had been about to say.

'Indian-lover?' Cyrus Hanley supplied. 'No, I ain't.' His tone was lemon bitter. 'But I can understand how a man who's had his land grabbed might feel wronged and hard-done-by.'

As they set off, Straker sat his saddle uneasy. He would have to trust Cyrus Hanley a whole lot more than he cared to. Though knowledgeable in reading sign and terrain, his know-how would not come anywhere near to matching Cyrus Hanley's, whose home as an outlaw were the canyons, ravines, creeks and draws of the vast land they were riding. Hanley, who had had a roof of stars for a long time would, should he be of a mind to use them, have a whole bag of tricks. He was a man hunted by Jack Galt and fear would be an ever-present factor, which could, despite Hanley's best intentions, decide his course of action when and if they came face to face with Galt. Dan's dark thoughts about how Hanley might lead them right to Galt returned to haunt him. The outlaw's recently uttered words rang hollowly in Straker's head.

'The young'r, the better Galt likes 'em.'

That would make the lovely Emily Clancy the trading chip of all trading chips!

CHAPTER FOURTEEN

Jack Galt could read sign with the crafty eye of an Indian, and what he was seeing pleased him.

'We're wastin' time, boss,' Raul Sanchez complained, the only man from whom Jack Galt would tolerate sass. 'We should be headed for Eagle Junction, pronto.'

Logically, Galt reasoned, 'Towns don't run away, Raul, my friend. Eagle Junction will still be there after I skin Hanley, and . . .' Galt examined the hoofprints in the sandy soil with eager interest, 'have the girl.'

Sanchez, no mean tracker himself, knew exactly the direction in which the gang-leader's thoughts would off-shoot, when he had seen the lighter hoof imprints compared to the accompanying heavier indentations.

'Might be a boy,' Sanchez ventured.

Galt shook his head with certainty. 'Two men,

one girl.' He grinned. 'If this is Hanley's sign,' Galt's finger followed the line of the lighter hoof imprint, 'looks like he's picked up mighty interesting company.'

Lewdly, Jack Galt massaged his private parts, his eyes taking on a dreamy, lustful look.

'Know an old miner's shack east of here,' Hanley said, as they rode on. 'It'll give shelter till the sun loses its anger. Got windows on all sides, too. That'll make it hard for critters to creep up on us.'

He veered off.

'But this is takin' us in the wrong direction, Dan,' Emily whined. 'What 'bout ma? She'll be sufferin' somethin' awful.'

'Sometimes,' Straker explained to the anxious girl, 'the longest way round can be faster, Emily.'

'That don't make sense, Dan,' Emily Clancy groused.

'In time, when you're fully grown—'

'I am fully growed!'

'It will,' Straker finished.

'Fancy talk,' Emily grumbled surlily. Dan Straker's heart pained him on seeing the wash of tears in Emily's eyes. 'You promised you'd help, Dan.'

Dan hated lying, but he saw no alternative to the untruth if mayhem was to be avoided. 'I'll get a doc and take him back to your ma, Emily.'

He hated himself even more when Emily

pleaded, 'Promise me, Dan.'

'I promise, Emily.'

Shit. It troubled Dan Straker that he could lie with such ease and sincerity.

An hour later, he irately questioned Cyrus Hanley: 'How far is this shack and how much off the Deepsville trail is it?'

'Only a coupla miles more,' came Hanley's answer. 'There's a back trail to Deepsville, an old Apache trail that we can take later. Ain't goin' to be in the best o' shape though, I reckon.' His eyes shifted Emily's way. 'Kinda winds round a canyon, too. Needs good horsemanship to stay in the saddle.'

Emily said spiritedly, 'Don't you worry none 'bout me, outlaw. I can ride through the eye of a darn needle, if needs be.' Emily's hand touched the Winchester in her saddle scabbard. 'You just be sure that you don't get no funny ideas 'bout comin' to a deal with this fella Galt.'

'Deal?' Hanley asked sourly. 'What kinda deal would that be, gal?'

Dan Straker thought about intervening to shut Emily up, but it was too late. Any intervention by him would only alert Cyrus Hanley to the fact that, like Emily, he had pondered on him betraying them as well. Emily's astuteness surprised Dan, which made it all the less understandable as to why she had not cottoned on to the yarn he had spun. But sometimes, he knew, that smart folk cottoned on to everything but what was most important of all to them, because they did not want to admit to what would hurt them most.

Emily elaborated: 'The kinda deal that would save your hide by handin' Dan and me over to this fella Galt to save your own scrawny neck, mister.'

The outlaw guffawed. 'Heck, Straker, you've got an imaginative one in tow there, fella.' He rode on, shaking his head as if the very idea was ludicrous in the extreme. But Straker had not missed the glint in the outlaw's eyes, and Dan knew that if he did not have the notion of trading them before, he certainly had now.

Dan's steely gaze made Emily aware of the blunder she had made, and all that he could hope for now was that it would not be a blunder that would prove fatal. Cyrus Hanley seemed a decent enough man; a man not in the traditional outlaw mode. But a man afraid was a man ready to betray.

St Peter had proved as much.

CHAPTER FIFTEEN

Mary Straker looked out of her bedroom window, her mood as black as a widow's weeds; a mood she had sunk deeper and deeper into since Dan's departure, or Josh, as she still thought of him in her private thoughts. So preoccupied in her gloomy disposition, she had not noticed the heavy black cloud rolling off the horizon. Or the second and even bigger cloud tumbling after it.

'Oh, Dan,' she murmured, 'come home safe. What would I do without you?'

There was a gentle knock on the bedroom door.

'Brought you some grub, Mary,' Arthur Flint called out. And as the time between his knock and Mary's response lengthened, 'You've got to eat something.'

'Just leave it outside, Arthur,' she called back.

'If that's what you want . . . .'

'That's what I want, Arthur.'

There was the clatter of a tray being placed on the ground outside the room door.

'Dan will be fine, Mary,' the storekeeper said. 'He's a wily one. He'll know what's best to do when the time comes, of that I have no doubt at all.'

'Hope so,' Mary called back.

Mary heard the creak of the stairs as Flint went below stairs. She slumped into a rocking chair near the window, still unsure as to how she felt about Arthur Flint and the people of Eagle Junction. She understood their fears, of course, but she could not understand them paying one man to probably sacrifice his life to save their own skins. It was a view she had hotly put to Flint and his fellow schemers shortly after Dan's departure.

'Just business, Mary,' was Saul Jennings, the Eagle Junction banker's explantion. 'Dan knows Jack Galt. That means he can get closer than most men to him.' His mood became sceptical. 'But I don't think Galt will listen to anything Dan has to say. I think once Dan gets close enough to Galt, he should kill him and be done with it!'

On seeing Mary's shock, he shrugged philosophically.

'If I needed a door made, I'd send for a carpenter. My horse shoed, a blacksmith. And a man killed, a fast gun.'

'If anything happens to, Dan,' Mary said, her mood sombre, 'I'll curse you all into the pit of hell!'

Flint had argued that they had handed Dan the chance to square his debts and keep his farm, but

Mary had responded bitterly, 'Never knew a dead man who worried about paying his debts, or a dead farmer who marshalled a plough horse.'

At first, Mary thought it was someone tapping at the window. Her first reaction was fear, thinking that it might be Dan's ghost. But then she saw the silver blobs on the window panes, more and more of them, and her heart sang out.

Rain!

Everything would be fine. However, her joy lasted only seconds. It was raining all right, but too late. Despondent, Mary sank back in her chair, with a new bitterness. Now she was angry with God, too.

'Not far now,' Cyrus Hanley promised, not for the first time. His eyes scanned ahead. 'Thing is, ev'ry-thin' looks purty much the same in this damn country.'

'Are you sayin' we're lost?' Emily Clancy asked bluntly.

'No, I ain't,' the outlaw whined.

Unforgiving, Emily snorted. 'Looks so to me.'

Emily exchanged an *I told you so* glance with Dan Straker. For the past hour of aimless wandering, Dan had begun to think that he had put all his eggs in the same basket as a lunatic. So he was mighty glad when Hanley yelped:

'Fat Nelly!'

His finger stabbed the air.

Dan looked to the boulders he was pointing to, and understood. On top of a large barrel-bellied boulder stood a neat round one, and it was not difficult to see in the arrangement the figure of a pregnant woman.

'A pard and me was holed up in the shack for a spell last fall, christened that rock Fat Nelly.'

'A good decription,' Dan agreed.

'The shack's just through that openin' up 'head.'

'Lead the way.'

As good as his word, five minutes later they were in a flat basin in which stood a shack that was so far gone that it even gave shacks a bad name.

'Never promised no Ritz!' Hanley grumbled, on seeing Straker's critical scrutiny of the shack.

But Dan's main concern sprang from the horse-shoe of high rocks overlooking the basin. True, the shack, as Hanley had promised, had windows on all sides, and there was clear ground around the rickety structure that would make it hard for a man to approach unseen, but an even average shooter would have no need to approach – he could pepper the shack from the high reaches of the canyon with little chance of anyone in the shack threatening him.

As they stepped inside the shack, the outlaw cautioned, 'Careful now. Rattlers. Nearly got one of them critter's fangs in my ass the time 'fore.'

They made slow progress. The place stunk of

recent occupation. Scraps of rotting food lay on the table and floor. Disturbed flies swarmed round them. Gagging, Emily said, 'I'd prefer to stay outside than use this hole for shade.'

'Wanna keep that purty hair of yours?' Hanley asked. Emily's hands went to her mane of blonde hair. 'Your maidenhood too, you'll stay put.'

Emily looked to Dan Straker. 'Cyrus is right, Emily. You'd be a prize that an Apache would find impossible to ignore.'

'Ain't no Indians in these parts, only tamed ones,' she protested.

'Hungry ones, too,' Dan said. 'Now don't give me any sass, Emily. Just do as you're darn well told!' In a kindlier tone, he added, 'No point in taking chances we don't have to take.'

Emily looked at him sulkily, but obeyed.

'Them cots might hide stinging or spitting critters,' Hanley warned.

Dan and the outlaw slowly lifted the greasy blankets, arching back from any possible strike by a snake, and were relieved to find only bed bugs crawling on the mattresses. They upended the cots and unloaded the crawlers as best they could.

'We'll rest in turns,' Dan told Hanley.

'I ain't bunkin' in no bug-infested cot,' Emily stated. 'Them critters can get in all sorts of places on a body.'

Dan Straker, a firm believer in cleanliness being next to godliness, sympathized with the girl. 'Ain't no bugs on the table,' he suggested.

Dan went outside and came back with the blanket from his bedroll. He swept away the scraps of rotting food on the table and laid the blanket on it to make the makeshift bed as comfortable as possible for Emily. He then went and leaned against the side of the south-facing window, the direction from which, he figured, trouble would come, *if* it came. 'I'll keep watch for the first hour,' he told Hanley, unnecessarily. The outlaw was already fast asleep.

During his watch, Dan frequently switched windows, watching all approaches to the shack as best he could. Coming to the end of his watch, Emily woke in the throes of a nightmare, fighting some imaginary demon. He calmed her and settled her down, but sleep for her was spoiled.

'Can I watch with you, Dan?' she asked. 'I got real good eyes.'

'Pretty, too,' Dan complimented. 'Be glad of the company, Emily.'

Jaded by the intense heat of the afternoon, Dan would have welcomed some shut-eye. But he could understand the girl's fear and loneliness. Theirs were compatible moods.

'Don't he ever get 'nuff o' women?' one of the Galt gang, a man called Myers moaned.

The man from Dakota had only joined the Galt outfit six weeks previously, and he was in awe of Jack Galt's appetite for females. Raul Sanchez said,

'You'll get used to the boss's ways soon enough, Myers,' and added ominously, 'If you live long enough, that is.'

Anger flared in Spike Myers' hollow eyes, but luckily for him he controlled his ire before his hand dived for his six gun. He'd have lost out to Sanchez, who, anticipating Myers' reaction, already had his .45 drawn, cocked and pointed.

The commotion attracted Jack Galt's attention. He had ridden ahead of the main party, anxious to get sight of the men and the girl. Finding empty and desolate country had not sweetened his humour, which had got steadily more dour and dangerous as his search for the girl grew longer. He swung about in his saddle, eyes burning.

'No problem, Jack,' Sanchez called to him. 'Just a small difference of opinion, amigo.'

Galt grunted, and resumed his perusal of the terrain.

Viciously, Raul Sanchez backhanded Myers. 'Keep your mouth shut and a clamp on your gunhand,' the Mexican warned Myers. 'If you know what's healthy for you, my friend.'

'I ain't scared of Galt or no man,' Myers irately flung back, but in a muted tone that would not carry to Galt, his defiance being purely to save face. He had been lucky, and knew it. He'd keep his mouth shut all right. The next sound from him that Galt and Sanchez would hear, would be the explosion of his gun some dark night.

Though Sanchez's and every other man's annoyance with Jack Galt was as keen as Myers' was, they knew better than to let it show. There was revenge to be taken for Ben Galt's life, sure enough, but, more important, there was likely a bulging bank vault to be emptied in Eagle Junction that would make life easy for a spell. Of late, the law had relentlessly dogged the gang's tail, and they had had a couple of close calls. There was also a rumour that the bankers and railroads had come together to organize a so-called super posse to run them to ground. That was worrying, and some of the gang were wishing for full pockets so that they could head out before that posse was formed. And maybe it had already been formed, which made a speedy conclusion of their business in Eagle Junction all the more urgent.

But Jack Galt had woman fever, and the only cure for that was the woman herself.

Dan Straker came awake with a start from the doze he had slipped into.

'It's OK, Dan,' Emily said, 'I've got him covered.'

'Him? Who?'

' 'Pache.'

'Alone?'

'Looks so.'

Dan edged his eye up to the window. It was as Emily said – the Indian was on his own, but Dan was slow to believe that. There would be others. The question was, how many? And where? Emily, though calm of body, could not conceal the fear in her eyes. She would have been loco, being a female and yellow haired, not to be afraid.

'Wait,' Dan said. 'Let's see what happens. Meanwhile . . .' Dan went and clamped his hand over Cyrus Hanley's mouth. 'Apaches,' he murmured. The outlaw's eyes glowed with fear. 'Only one for now,' he answered in reply to the question in Hanley's eyes.

'Ain't never only one,' Hanley gasped, when Dan took his hand from over his mouth.

Dan, back at the window, swung angrily about as Hanley, getting out of bed, snagged his foot on his blanket and crashed to the shack floor.

'Gone!' Emily said, leaning out the window.

Dan hauled her back inside.

Misinterpreting his concern for anger, Emily apologized, 'Only blinked and he vanished, Dan.'

'Shit!' Hanley wailed. 'Now that he's seen them yellow plaits o' yours, we're in deep trouble, girl.'

'Leave her alone,' Straker defended Emily. 'She didn't know what she was doing.'

Sourly, the outlaw griped, 'Deep trouble, I tell ya.'

An hour had passed. There was no sign of the Apaches.

'Mebbe they're gone,' Emily hoped.

'They ain't gone nowhere,' Cyrus Hanley crankily assured the girl. 'They'll sit and wait. 'Paches got the kinda patience that drives a man insane. And they'll be more patient now that they know there's a woman in here.'

His sour-faced gaze settled on Emily. Straker was about to tell Hanley to lay off the girl, but he held his tongue. He could understand the outlaw's sense of grievance. He was right, Emily's instinctive reaction to the Indian's disappearance had landed them with a predicament that might prove to be their undoing.

Only time would tell.

CHAPTER SIXTEEN

Another half-hour was torturously spent before Dan Straker told the outlaw with weary resignation, 'I guess one of us is going to have to show himself, to test their intentions.'

Cyrus Hanley's eyes popped with new fear.

'Have you got a better idea?' Dan asked.

The outlaw licked parched lips, and let his gaze drift Emily Clancy's way. Dan could see the wheels turning in the outlaw's head. He waited. The wheels stopped, and Hanley turned to Straker.

'Guess not,' he said.

Cyrus Hanley went up a notch in Dan Straker's reckoning, for discounting the obvious solution of trading the girl for their hides. Of course, the outlaw might have figured that such a suggestion would bring a quick and furious reaction from him, which it would have. But Dan thought that that was not the way of it, based on the look of revulsion and self-loathing on Hanley's face.

Straker's fear was as keen as Hanley's at the prospect of stepping out of the shack, but his hands did not shake as much. If the outlaw went outside and there was a need for a fast and accurate gun, it would be a miracle if he were to puncture anything but air.

'Be back in no time at all, Emily,' Dan promised. 'Meanwhile, I reckon that Mr Hanley will take good care of you.'

Emily fretted, 'You're goin' to leave me all 'lone with an outlaw, Dan?'

Straker said, 'Emily, some men are outlaws by nature and kind. Other men fall into bad ways through misfortune and cruel fate.' He looked steadily at Cyrus Hanley. 'Like Mr Hanley, I figure.'

At the shack door, Dan tensed and readied himself to spring.

'I'll cover you as best I can,' Cyrus Hanley promised.

'I'm sure you will, Cyrus.' His glance went to Emily. 'Be sure to take good care of the girl.'

The unspoken message in Dan Straker's eyes, asking Hanley not to let Emily fall into Apache hands should the worse happen, understood and agreed, Dan sprinted from the shack. The next couple of seconds might stop him dead in his tracks.

Raul Sanchez let out a yell that brought Jack Galt up short. He grabbed the blue ribbon snagged on a bush and held it aloft. Galt swung about and galloped back up out of the creek to take the ribbon from the Mexican, his fingers toying with the entangled blonde hairs.

Galt charged to the exit from the creek where the sandy soil showed three sets of hoofs – the same as he had seen earlier, a V shaped nick from one hoof showing clearly. Galt was elated, because on the stony approach to the creek, from about a mile back, the tracks had disappeared and he feared that he would not pick them up again.

He looked to the country ahead and correctly guessed, 'They're headed for Deepsville.' Again he examined the tracks. 'The prints are fresh. They can't be far ahead.'

He laughed harshly.

'I'm going to have me that girl tonight, Raul.'

CHAPTER SEVENTEEN

As he sprinted from the shack, Dan Straker's eyes flashed every which way. He dived to the ground, his rifle stalking the high rocks, from where he reckoned the threat to him would be keenest. He was well within rifle range, and even in danger from a skilled bowman. Another problem for Dan were the blindspots created by the intense glare of the sun in his eyes, because from such a blindspot might come the bullet or arrow that would claim him.

Seconds as long as weeks ticked by.

Shale slithered down from high up, setting up a discordant, unnerving music. Dan, figuring the spill of shale might be a ruse to engage his attention on that spot while trouble sprang from another, kept his eyes scanning as much of the terrain as was possible. The Apache was a master at getting a man to look one way, while he crept up on him from another direction.

'See anything?' Dan called back to the shack.

'Nothin',' came back Hanley's reply.

Straker did not see the Apache creeping from a hole in the ground behind him, concealed by desert weed. What Dan did not know was, that under the basin there existed a network of shafts, some natural, more man-made, dug out by the Apaches and used by them in their battles with the army and other intruders. Many men, as unsuspecting as Dan, unaware of the basin's underfoot treachery, had paid with their lives.

As the Apache crept up, knife poised to slit Dan Straker's throat, it looked like he was going to pay with his life too. He was ready to loop his arm around Dan's neck when, from high up in the rocks, a rifle spat to shatter the Indian's spine. Suddenly the basin was crawling with Indians. It seemed every boulder and rock hid one, where only seconds before there was nothing to be seen, proving the Apache to be masters of subterfuge.

It was only a short sprint back to the shack, but Dan doubted if he would make it.

CHAPTER EIGHTEEN

Under a hail of lead, Dan was mindful of the fact that friendly fire was every bit as deadly as enemy fire. The air was filled, too, with the *whoosh* of arrows. Two Indians desperate to nail Dan, leaped on top of twin boulders. He spun round to blast one, while the second Apache fell to his unknown benefactor.

Emily, at the shack door, dropped an Indian about to leap on Dan, tomahawk ready to open his skull. From a window, Cyrus Hanley's gun spoke and another two died. The mysterious shooter's bullets strafed the basin, and sent the remaining Apaches dodging for cover. Four more were felled by the unknown and unseen rifleman.

Dan murmured, 'Glad you're on my side, friend.'

The Indians scattered. Seconds later the sound of galloping ponies announced their departure. All except one lust-driven buck still in hiding who charged the shack, prepared to risk forfeiting his life to get his hands on Emily Clancy. Dan triggered the Winchester and heard the hollow sound of an empty gun. Off balance, the charging Indian had little difficulty in bungling Dan over. Straker grabbed at the Apache's ankles. The Indian stumbled. Dan swung out a leg and his boot caught the Apache on the thigh, lower than he had aimed for, but the hefty blow still buckled his right leg. Dan quickly followed through with a pile-driver to the Indian's head, but as he shot backwards from the force of Straker's blow a knife flashed in his hand. An athletic spin brought him into a crouch, knife slashing, forcing Dan to dance away from him. Dan's hand dived for his six gun, to find an empty holster. The gun lay about twenty feet away, but there was no way that he'd get to it before the Indian got to him. Anyway, all the Apache had to do was throw the knife. The Indian had also cunningly positioned Dan between him and the shack, constantly adjusting his stance to keep it that way. If Emily or Hanley tried to shoot the Apache, they would have to risk hitting Dan.

Dan adjusted his eyes when, from the side of the shack a strange apparition wearing tails and a stovepipe hat appeared, rifle hip-high and spitting. The buck pitched forward, eyes vacant.

'Howdy, folks,' the strangely attired gent, with the crowbait visage greeted.

'Doc Fanshaw!' Emily raced from the shack to the man's arms.

'Why, if it isn't Emily Clancy.' The shooter's greeting of Emily was every bit as warm as hers for him. His glance went to Straker and Hanley, and his rifle came level with them. 'What the devil are you doing way out here, Emily, girl?'

Dan Straker answered, 'I'm taking Emily to Deepsville to get help for her ma.'

'What kind of help would that be?' Fanshaw questioned closely, still covering them with his rifle.

Emily burst into tears. 'Ma's bust her leg, Doc. Dan is helping me to get help for her.'

'Busted her leg, you say? When would that have been, Emily?'

'Almost a week 'go, Doc. I splinted ma's leg as best I know how.'

Horace Fanshaw ruffled Emily Clancy's blonde hair, like a kindly grandfather might. 'And a fine job you did too, I bet.'

Emily grinned. 'You reckon, Doc?'

'I reckon, girl.'

Fanshaw's gaze went beyond Emily to Dan Straker. Dan shook his head.

'Where's Rosita, Doc?' Emily eagerly enquired.

'Why, right here, Emily.'

Horace Fanshaw whistled and a wagon rumbled through the entrance to the canyon. When the wagon reached Fanshaw, the horse nuzzled him fondly. The medico explained, 'This here is Rosita, folks.' The horse neighed. 'Rosita says that she's mighty pleased to make your acquaintance.'

Emily laughed. 'You sayin' you understand horse talk, Doc.'

'Every word,' Fanshaw assured Emily.

'Ah, Doc,' she giggled.

Fondly rubbing Rosita's neck, Fanshaw told Straker and Hanley, 'Named this kind-hearted creature after a comely maiden whose company I once shared for a spell south of the border.' His deep, reflective sigh told them that he had enjoyed the woman's company. 'Went back when I realized how foolish I'd been in leaving.' His crowbait face became bleak with remembrance. 'Found her boxed and ready for burying. She refused Jack Galt's advances. He slit her throat.'

His eyes became as hard as flint.

'That was a year ago. Been looking to even the score with Galt ever since. That man's got his stamp on every rotten deed in these parts.' He shook his head. 'Jack Galt's the Devil's Disciple, for sure.'

Fanshaw looked curiously at Straker and Hanley. 'What're you fellas doing in this country?'

Straker replied, 'I'm searching for Jack Galt, too.'

'I'm running from Jack Galt,' Hanley added.

Fanshaw chuckled. 'Seems that there's a whole passel of people who Galt has upset.'

Emily tugged at Horace Fanshaw's tail coat. 'What 'bout ma, Doc?'

'I was just on my way to see your ma, Emily,' the medico declared. He rubbed his slack belly. 'I was hoping to fill this hole inside me that keeps rattling, before I cross the Rio Grande.'

'Did you see any sign of Galt in your travels, Doc?' Dan quizzed.

Fanshaw said sombrely, 'If I had one of two things would have happened. I wouldn't be standing here gabbing to you fellas. Or Jack Galt would be buzzard bait.' The sawbones opined: 'In this vastness, if you don't know where to find a man, you could wander for ever and not cross trails with him. Finding Galt is like finding that needle in the haystack, mister.'

Dan held out his hand to shake.

'Dan Straker's the name, Doc.'

Fanshaw shook Dan's hand, his eyes suddenly alert. 'Straker, huh? Ever been to Quido, Mr Straker?'

Cyrus Hanley yelped, 'Quido?' He spun around on Dan. 'You're Josh Lawson, ain't ya?' Dan saw no point in denying the outlaw's assertion. 'Your dial's been twiggin' at me since I first laid eyes on you. You've changed a whole lot in the years since you vanished from Quido, sure 'nuff. But those eyes, once looked into proper, ain't forgotten.' He confessed: 'I was on my way into the Quido Cattlemen's Bank to rob it, and you were on your way out. I never forgot the message in those eyes of yours. It said: Don't even think 'bout it, mister.'

'Saw a dust trail about an hour ago . . .' Attention was back on Horace Fanshaw.

'Not Indians, I reckon. The dust cloud was too thin.' He elaborated with the ease of a man well grounded in knowledge and experience, 'Apaches come with a string of ponies in tow, the spent ones they eat. Yes, sir, Indians raise a whole lot of dust. These riders' progress was ponderous.'

'Ponderous?' Straker questioned.

'Yes. Breaks in the dust cloud. I reckon these fellas were checking for sign.'

'Lawmen or bounty hunters, maybe?' Hanley suggested, uneasily.

'Could be,' Fanshaw agreed. 'Or outlaws.'

Cyrus Hanley gulped. 'The Galt gang?'

'Could you tell the riders' direction from the dust plume?' Dan anxiously asked Fanshaw.

'That's sure a skill, Mr Straker. But . . . well, I reckon they were headed Deepsville way. In fact they shouldn't be too far behind me.'

Dan's relief was palpable. 'It's not the Galt gang, then.'

'Oh?'

'If Jack Galt is on the move, he'd be headed to Eagle Junction.'

'Why Eagle Junction?' Fanshaw asked.

Straker filled the medico in on the happenings in Eagle Junction, and saw no point in holding back on his reason for seeking out Jack Galt. The sawbones' reaction was a bemused one.

'Get Jack Galt to change his mind about mayhem?' he mused. 'Don't waste your time, Straker. If Galt's got killing on his mind, then killing it will surely be.'

'Told ya, Dan,' Cyrus Hanley pronounced. 'Tanglin' with Galt is like puttin' your hand into a hole fulla rattlers. In fact, doin' that would be less risky than tryin' to reason with Jack Galt!'

'Doc, can we go see ma now?' Emily Clancy pleaded.

'Sure. But we need to get grub, Emily. It's a goodly trek back to your ma, and you look piquey, girl. Don't want you folding on me.'

'Ah, I'm as tough as old boots, Doc.'

'Still . . . .'

During the hastily prepared and meagre meal, Horace Fanshaw settled down alongside Dan Straker. 'How bad is Elinora Clancy, Straker?' He smiled. 'Guess you don't want to be called Lawson, huh?'

Dan's shoulders slumped. 'With half the darn country knowing by now that I'm Josh Lawson, don't see that it makes a whole lot of difference, Doc.'

'A man's got a right to his privacy, I say.'

Sombrely, Dan replied, 'Not a man like me, Doc.'

'You'll find that privacy again, when all this is over,' Fanshaw predicted. 'Now, about Elinora Clancy's injury?'

'I don't figure on you finding her alive,' was Dan Straker's opinion. 'And if you do, she'll not be far from passing over, I reckon.'

'What were your plans for Emily in Deepsville?'

'I was hoping to place her with a kind and caring family. Maybe with a woman who can't have children of her own.'

Dan's thoughts went to Mary, and her disappointment at not being able to present him with a son, or a couple of boys – daughters, too.

Fanshaw stood up, and threw away the dregs of his coffee. 'If you find Jack Galt before I do, Straker, put a bullet in his belly for me.'

'If I shoot him,' Dan said.

Horace Fanshaw said, 'Get it through your head, mister. You'll have to shoot him, for sure.' He walked off a couple of paces, paused and turned. 'That is, *if* you can shoot him.'

The medico pondered.

'A lot of shooting just now. Gunfire attracts attention. Be wary, Straker.'

CHAPTER NINETEEN

'Riders coming,' the man in the church steeple hollered.

After their initial joy on seeing the drought break, the downpour had forced the citizens of Eagle Junction back indoors. However, Luke Bradford's holler from the church steeple had doors opening again, fear-filled eyes peering out.

'How many riders, Luke?' Arthur Flint called out to Bradford.

'Hard to say, Mr Flint, with the rain blurring ev'rything the way it is.'

'Maybe three,' a man positioned on the roof of the hotel, which was further along the street, called out.

Three did not make a gang. To try and stem the rising panic, Flint said as much. But the common view was that the approaching riders were only the vanguard of the Galt gang.

'Looks like our scheme went up in smoke,' Saul

Jennings the bank president grumbled. 'And two thousand dollars with it!'

'I guess it was a long shot anyway,' Charles Wayne, the town lawyer, who was one of the quartet of businessmen who had drawn up the plan to use Dan Straker's services, said regretfully, his frame of mind more philosophical than the banker's.

'You're not the custodian of a bank vault, Charlie,' Jennings snapped, and added spitefully, 'but I guess the Galt gang will take your money along with the rest of the town's cash.'

Alarmed, the shyster begged Flint, 'You've got to do something, Arthur. And fast!'

The fourth member of the quartet, Samuel Levridge broke ranks, hurrying away.

'Where are you headed, Sam?' Flint enquired.

'The livery, first,' he flung back. 'Then the bank.'

'An odd time to be doing business, Sam,' Jennings opined.

'It'll be short and none too sweet, Saul,' Levridge said snappily. 'Doesn't take much time to close an account. I'll be by in ten minutes at most.'

'You're running out?' Flint sneered.

'You bet I am,' Levridge growled. 'By the time Galt gets through, this burg will be a mound of smouldering ashes.'

Quickening his pace, Levridge made tracks to the livery.

Flint and his remaining partners exchanged urgent glances, their thoughts in tune. It was Jennings who voiced those thoughts.

'Maybe Sam is talking sense,' he suggested.

'Guess he might be at that,' the storekeeper agreed.

Wayne said, 'It isn't just the money. We've got a right and duty to protect ourselves.'

Coming to the point, Saul Jennings said, 'We'll all meet up at the bank in ten minutes.'

They were hurrying away to gather together what they could, when Wayne advised, 'Best to leave town one at a time, I figure. All leaving together would cause a stir.'

'Time is on the short side,' Flint cautioned. He called up to the church steeple, 'How far away are those riders now, Luke?'

'Not far, Mr Flint. I reckon we should be getting more men with guns on the rooftops.'

'Maybe if we did just that we could—'

'Forget it!' The storekeeper dismissed the lawyer's idea out of hand. 'Galt's outfit are hard-bitten fighters.' Scoffing, he glanced about the town. 'Each man here will be shooting in hope instead of certainty. And most, I reckon, will high-tail it like us when the air buzzes with lead.'

'Running out on your neighbours with bulging pockets isn't the gentlemanly thing to do.' They swung around. Mary Straker stepped from the door of Flint's store, holding a Winchester. By way of explantion, she said, 'Figured you fellas were up to no good, huddled like you were.'

Flint was first to find his tongue. 'Why, Mary, you've got a wrong handle on this,' he said, suavely.

'Don't reckon I have, Arthur,' Mary said uncompromisingly. 'And I also reckon that you gents should stay right here in town with the rest of us folk.'

Flint persisted, 'Like I said, Mary. You've got this all wr—'

'Oh, shut up, Flint!' Jennings snarled. He addressed Mary Straker, 'You can continue to hold us under threat of that rifle, ma'am,' he stated, businesslike. 'Or you can throw your lot in with us.'

Mary feigned interest. 'Go on, Mr Jennings.'

Confident that he had roped Mary into their skullduggery, he went on, 'A thousand dollars on top of what we paid your husband. Nice penny, I'd say.'

Flint and Wayne leaned on each other for support.

'Interesting,' was Mary Straker's comment.

'But, as you can observe, Mrs Straker,' Jennings said, 'we've got to be quick about this.' He ran a finger inside a collar that was getting tighter by the second. 'Those riders are getting nearer all the time.'

'Mighty tempting,' was Mary's comment.

Arthur Flint was stunned. There was no accounting for human nature. Mary Straker, selling out? What next?

'But . . . .'

Jennings did not waste time haggling. Mary Straker had them over a barrel. 'Two thousand.'

Flint gulped. Wayne swayed.

'It's a lot of cash,' the banker coaxed.

'Surely is,' Mary agreed. 'But it might be the honest thing to do to just let the good folk of this town know about—'

'Honesty doesn't line your pockets,' the banker interjected.

Mary Straker considered the banker for a long moment. 'I guess that explains why yours are bulging fit to burst, Saul.'

A spark of anger flared in the banker's muddy eyes, but he held his temper in check.

To Arthur Flint's amazement, Mary said, 'Shall we head for the bank, gents?'

Pleased as punch, Saul Jennings crooned, 'Lead the way, Mary. But I suggest that you hide that Winchester under your petticoats.' His smirk was rifely sarcastic. 'We wouldn't want someone thinking that you were trying to rob the bank now, would we?'

'Under my petticoats, this rifle would be difficult to retrieve in time if you gents were to change your minds and decide to end our, ah . . .' Mary Straker's smile was the kind a cat has after a saucer of cream, '*arrangement.*'

Flint was outraged. 'Mary! We're men of our word.'

Mary snorted. 'Who are about to hightail it and save your hides at everyone else's expense. Which, frankly, Arthur,' Mary bluntly stated, 'makes you gentlemen no gentlemen at all.'

While Flint and Wayne blustered, Saul Jennings had his eye on an upcoming alley. On reaching it, for a big-bellied man, he moved swiftly to bundle Mary into the alley with the black-hearted intention of doing her grievous harm, but she niftily side-stepped and left the banker clutching air. Incensed by his trickery, Mary almost triggered the Winchester.

'Easy now, Mary,' Jennings urged, his jowly face suddenly beaded with perspiration. 'Don't be hasty. There's still that pile of money to be had.'

'Heh, Mr Flint,' the man on the hotel roof called out, 'those riders are gettin' real close.'

'Say something,' Wayne urged the tongue-tied storekeeper, as the seconds mounted up without a response from him.

Gasping, Flint croaked, 'We're dr-drawing up a p-plan, Bob.'

'Better make it fast,' Luke Bradford in the church steeple called down, and added, 'and good, too.'

'And I hope it ain't as air-headed as your last scheme to stop Galt, Flint,' another unidentified male voice hollered.

'Yeah,' another man said, angrily. 'Prob'ly got Galt more riled than ever!'

'Best make fast tracks,' Mary Straker advised.

Seemingly content now to hand over the money, the banker was in fact seething. Saul Jennings spent the minute it took to reach the bank thinking faster than a rattler's fangs. The derringer pistol inside the bank vault gave him as much warm comfort as a wool blanket would a down-and-out on a snowy night. It used to be a Colt .45, but every time he opened the vault he shivered on seeing the gun, and had a secret fear that by some cruel twist of fate that one day he would open the vault and the gun would blast him.

It seemed that the devil was looking after his own when, only a couple of days previously, he had switched the .45 for the derringer. The ladygun would not create the hole in Mary Straker that the Colt would have, more's the pity. However, close up, and ruthlessly used, the gun would still Mary's tongue. Another fortuitous break was that the derringer's blast would likely not be heard outside the bank. And if it were, its sound could be put down to many things in the panic gripping the town. Unlike the the blast of a Colt .45, the derringer's less robust explosion would not be as familiar, and infinitely less intrusive.

Arriving at the bank door, Jennings stepped aside to usher Mary inside.

CHAPTER TWENTY

Jack Galt slid back from the ledge, his smile leery, his eyes wild with desire.

'Well?' Raul Sanchez asked.

Galt sneered. 'Pretty, young and ripe, Raul.'

'How many guns?' one of the gang, a polecat mean-mouthed man asked.

'Four,' Galt answered.

'Four!' the man groused.

Galt elaborated, 'Hanley, Doc Fanshaw—'

'Fanshaw?' Sanchez asked, worriedly, only too aware of the medico's gun prowess.

Annoyed by the interruption, Jack Galt growled, 'The girl—'

'The girl?' the mean-mouthed man griped.

'Shoots nearly as good as Fanshaw does,' Galt said, with a glint of admiration and lots more. 'And, a fella by the name of Josh Lawson.'

The gang members were knocked back in their saddles. Each man had heard tales, some tall, some true, about the Quido marshal and how hard men gave the border town a wide berth while he was the badge-toter there.

'Thought he was dead?' Sanchez said.

'Are you sure it's Lawson?' another man quizzed Galt.

'I'm sure,' the gang leader confirmed. 'No mistaking Josh Lawson. He saved my life once.'

Sanchez said, 'That makes you beholden, Jack.'

Jack Galt's eyes frosted over. 'If he stands between me and the girl . . . .'

On hearing the wheels of Fanshaw's wagon crunching gravel, Galt belly-crawled to the edge of the ledge and tensed with alarm. 'Fanshaw and the girl are moving out! Sanchez,' he barked, 'it's time to use that old ruse that your cousin Miguel told us about.'

Raul Sanchez smiled.

Quickly, Galt took a broken arrow from his saddle bag and a pouch of red dye which he liberally applied to Sanchez's left side. Then the Mexican tore his shirt and dirtied his face to give the impression of a man who has been through a skirmish with the Indians. He poured the red dye over his right hand. He made his way cautiously down from the ledge, slouched in the saddle and holding the broken arrow against his side. The ruse which his bandit cousin Miguel had used many times, never failed. Westerners always welcomed a wounded man into their midst. And once inside . . . .

Sanchez slanted his head sideways, using the brim of his hat to cover most of his face from view. As he drew nearer there was a chance that Cyrus Hanley would recognize him as Jack Galt's enforcer.

'There's four of 'em,' Luke Bradford hailed from the church steeple.

'And they're sittin' mean in the saddle,' the man on the hotel roof added.

'You know, gents,' Mary Straker said cordially 'I think it best if I wait right here while you go and fetch the cash.'

Saul Jennings grinned amiably. 'Why, Mary. Don't you trust us?'

To which Mary answered bluntly, 'No. I don't. Not for one second. You're a cautious and clever man Jennings, and I'm betting that in that safe of yours, you've got a surprise.'

Flint's and Wayne's eyes flashed the banker's way. Confidants of the banker, they knew Jennings had a derringer planted in the bank safe. But would he use it on Mary Straker? His cold-eyed glance ended their speculation.

Mock shock registered on Saul Jennings' face. 'Mary, my dear, you think—?'

Mary scoffed. 'Look at it this way. I'm just removing temptation from your reach.'

'Darn, Flint,' the look-out in the church steeple

complained, 'where's that damn plan you fellas've have been hatchin'?'

The Galt outfit readied themselves. Sanchez was well inside the enemy camp. Josh Lawson was coming to meet what he thought to be a stricken man. Fanshaw was less eager, holding back. Cyrus Hanley's curiosity was aroused, but he bided his time.

Raul Sanchez had his eye on Hanley, because he reckoned the outlaw was on the verge of recognizing him.

'Satisfied?' Saul Jennings snarled, as he handed over to Mary Straker a cloth sack of dollar bills. 'Now can we get on with our own business?'

Mary felt the sack, and for the briefest moment she was tempted. The stash could solve all of hers and Dan's problems. She had by now decided to leave, and to not take no for an answer from Dan on his return – if he returned. There was no future here. One good crop would be followed by a couple of bad yields. Dan was placing his hope in the diversion of the mountain stream, but Mary was not as hopeful. The water would have to come a long way, along a thirsty track that would soak it up and, in Mary's opinion, leave little to bring life to their fields. No, as soon as Dan got back, she'd hitch a wagon and shake the dust of Eagle Junction from their heels.

'Sorry, gents,' she said. 'You're not going anywhere.'

'Bitch!' Jennings swore, and dived for the derringer he had pocketed from the bank safe.

Mary shot him in the chest. All eyes swung the bank's way, as Saul Jennings toppled into the muddy street and lay still in the downpour. Mary held the cloth sack aloft. 'There's a full explanation in this sack,' she told the townsfolk.

Knowing the game was up, Levridge made good use of the confusion. He burst from the livery, setting a breakneck pace out of town. A mile on, head still down and galloping, Levridge crossed paths with the three riders approaching town and knew how stupid he had been when he recognized the riders as Sam Burns' rannies.

CHAPTER TWENTY-ONE

As Cyrus Hanley stepped forward, his scrutiny of Sanchez getting ever keener, the Mexican let himself topple from his horse.

'Doc,' Straker called, grabbing Sanchez to break his fall.

Hanley exclaimed, just a second too late, 'Dan, that's Raul Sanchez. Jack Galt's henchman!'

Dan felt the prod of a knife in his belly. 'Easy,' Sanchez advised. 'You'd be dead by now if you hadn't saved Jack Galt's life. But I guess now you can take it that accounts have been settled.' He stepped behind Dan and looped an arm around his neck, transferring the threat of the knife to his spine. 'One little jerk and you're a dead man, Lawson.'

Fanshaw and Hanley were caught cold by the Mexican's swiftness.

Appearing on the ledge above, Jack Galt

ordered, 'Throw your guns to Sanchez.'

Horace Fanshaw instantly complied. 'Ain't no fight of mine, Mr Galt. I just stopped by to help these fellas with some Apache raiders.'

'Bastard!' Cyrus Hanley spat.

Fanshaw snorted. 'It's not my hide that's for skinning, mister.'

'How could you do this, Doc?' Emily Clancy accused the medico, struggling to believe what she had just witnessed.

'Sensible move,' Galt congratulated the sawbones. Turning his attention to Cyrus Hanley he repeated, 'The gun. Now!'

Hanley thought about trying to shoot Raul Sanchez, but being slimmer than Dan Straker and cleverly using the farmer's bulk to hide behind, even an ace shooter would need all the luck that was going to even wing Sanchez. He fought to bring his fear under control. On balance, while he remained breathing, a chance might present itself to turn the tables. He vowed that should Fanshaw be still standing with him after the encounter, he'd make damn sure that the sawbones paid for his treachery. He slung his rifle to join Fanshaw's at Raul Sanchez's feet.

'The girl's rifle!' Galt barked. 'I've seen how that girly can shoot. And six guns, too.'

Emily had put her rifle on the seat of Fanshaw's wagon, ready to leave for home.

'Sure thing, Mr Galt,' Fanshaw said. He

collected the rifle and added it to his and Hanley's.

Emily Clancy's fists hammered on the medico's chest in anger. 'I'm goin' to kill ya, Doc,' she promised. Galt disappeared from the ledge. Shortly, the gang joined Sanchez, six all told.

Horace Fanshaw had the information he needed.

Saul Jennings was dead. Sam Levridge was on the run without a cent to his name, and dared not come back to town to claim his fortune. Arthur Flint and Charles Wayne were in the town jail, all for nothing. There was no sign of the Galt gang.

Mary Straker spoke up for Flint, pointing out how he had helped a lot of struggling folk during the drought, and putting the case that his lapse into treachery had been through fear (which everyone understood, feeling it themselves), rather than any intentional malice. Her eloquent and passionate defence of the storekeeper softened the town's ugly mood towards Flint.

'Now,' she told the hastily-convened citizens' committee, 'I'm going home to wait for Dan's arrival.'

'Wouldn't you be safer here in town until this whole affair is decided?' one of committee opined.

'I always told Dan that if he was abroad I'd keep a light in the window to light his last few steps home. It's a promise I'm going to keep.'

*

149

Jack Galt stepped down from his horse to face Josh Lawson. Sanchez had stepped aside, now that Galt guns had the gathering covered.

'Josh,' he greeted. 'It's been a long time. Thought you were dead.'

'It's what I hoped most folk would believe, Jack,' Dan replied.

'What're you doing in this country?' Galt enquired.

'I was looking for you.'

'Me?' Galt sneered. 'You're not toting a badge again, are you?'

'No. I'm a farmer now.'

'Suits, I guess,' was Galt's opinion. 'Married that pretty Union nurse, didn't you?'

'Yes. Mary Duff did me the honour of becoming my wife.'

Jack Galt grinned wolfishly. 'Always liked pretty women, Josh.' His glance slid Emily Clancy's way. 'Young and pretty is better still.'

It was in that moment that Dan Straker realized that it was as everyone had said it would be. There would be no hope of persuading Jack Galt to do anything other than what he wanted. And right now his needs were crystal clear.

Galt swung back to Straker.

'Looking for me, you said, Josh. Why?'

'I live in Eagle Junction . . . .'

Galt's face became granite. 'Hope you had nothing to do with Ben's murder?'

150

'I was hoping to talk you out of taking revenge on the town.'

'You didn't answer my question, Josh.'

'No's the answer.'

'Good. As to not taking revenge for Ben's death . . .' he raised his hands in the air, 'what kind of brother would I be if I didn't, Josh?'

Horace Fanshaw stumbled backwards, making some kind of animal sound. He crashed to the ground alongside his medicine wagon, eyes rolling, breath heaving.

'What's wrong with him?' one of the gang asked.

'Looks like a fit of some kind,' Galt pronounced. 'Let him be. He'll pull through or die. Don't care much either way.'

Fanshaw, legs and arms jerking went rigid. He lay still, eyes open and vacant.

Galt laughed. 'Guess the doc didn't make it, fellas.'

The gang joined in Galt's cruel laughter. His gaze swept Emily and Hanley. He told Dan, 'You can ride out of here, Josh.' He then chillingly stated, 'Hanley, I'm going to skin alive. The girl, I aim to have.'

'Then I guess you'll have to kill me too, Jack,' Dan Straker said with steely resolve. 'Because if you let me ride, I'll dog your trail until I square accounts!'

Galt snorted. 'Always full of Southern honour, weren't you, Josh?' He looked to the sky where

151

long fingers of approaching night were spreading across it. 'Tell you what, Josh. I'll give you . . . oh, five minutes to change your mind. By then, if you still carry on with this noble shit, I'll kill you. And it will be no one's fault but your own.'

Horace Fanshaw rolled a careful eye to the rifle strapped under the medicine wagon. If Galt could use a ruse, so could he. It wasn't the first time he had had a convenient fit. And it seemed that he was as good an actor as he was a sawbones. His problem now was in reaching for the rifle. The wagon was tilted away from him, and he would have to roll under it to grab the rifle.

All he could count on was that, being a dead man and no threat, eyes would be averted. But once the surprise of his ressurrection was over-come, which would be mere seconds, every Galt gun would be blasting his way.

Surprise was a powerful tool. As Horace Fanshaw dived for the hidden rifle, be prayed that the seconds that surprise would give him, would be enough.

CHAPTER TWENTY-TWO

Raul Sanchez was quickest to react, his six gun leaving leather lightning quick. Fanshaw felt the breeze of his bullet on his left cheek, but he had the rifle in his grasp and two of the Galt gang were already hellbound.

Cyrus Hanley dived for his rifle. Another Galt man folded. Sanchez rounded. Hanley cried out, his shoulder shattered, his gunhand useless. The Mexican was lining Hanley up for the kill when Dan Straker lunged at him, and swung the Mexican round just in time to get Jack Galt's bullet in the head. Then Emily Clancy had Galt dancing with the bullets biting the ground around him.

The one Galt man standing, other than Galt himself, tossed his pistol aside and threw up his hands.

Dan Straker picked up his six gun and holstered it. 'I made a mistake in saving your rotten hide,

Galt,' he grated. 'Now I guess all I can do is right that wrong.'

Horace Fanshaw restrained Emily.

'But Galt is snake-spit fast, Doc,' she protested.

'It's the way it's got to be, Emily. Right from the second Josh Lawson saved Galt's life, it was always probably going to come down to this.'

'I'm faster, Josh,' Galt said.

'Maybe. Maybe not.'

Dan noted with hope the slight tremor in Jack Galt's legs.

'I guess there's only one way to find out, Galt.'

As they faced each other both men pondered on their chances, and both of them were finding that it was true that all of a man's life flashed past in the final seconds of his life. Seconds as heavy as lead ticked by. Buzzards, anticipating a feast, had taken up a grim vigil on the high reaches of the canyon.

Galt and Straker dived for their guns. Both guns exploded together. Both men were still standing. Then, Jack Galt bent over. He could hear cannon fire. Men screaming. The stench of death was everywhere. It caught in his throat. He could see a tattered flag in the mud. A man in grey was crawling towards it, trying to raise it again. A man – no a mere boy, came out of the smoke, weapon raised. He was in his sights. Then the boy was spun backwards. His life had been saved.

Now Jack Galt looked up at the man he knew as Josh Lawson. He sighed. 'I guess it would have been better if you'd let me die that night, Josh,' he murmured. 'I might not have been damned.'

He folded.

Emily ran to Dan's arms, cheering. Gently, he told her, 'A man's death is not something to rejoice over, Emily.'

It was night, two days later, when Mary Straker heard the rumble of a wagon arriving in the yard. She ran to the window, her face lit by the lamp's yellow light, and peered into the darkness. She saw a medicine wagon, driven by a crow-bait, lanky, tail-coated man, wearing a stovepipe hat. A young girl and a man with his arm in a sling shared the wagon seat with him. But her curiosity was quickly replaced by joy when she saw the familiar gait of the rider coming out of the darkness behind the wagon. She raced outside, dragged Dan from the saddle, and held him tighter than she'd ever held him before, even in the passion-heady days of courtship and honeymoon. When he finally broke free of her frenzied hug, he introduced her visitors.

Come morning, Horace Fanshaw departed. Dan and Mary had spoken long into the night, and after breakfast had put it to the orphan, Emily Clancy, that she might want to be their daughter – a proposition which Emily gleefully accepted.

Two weeks later, Dan and Mary Straker rolled out of Eagle Junction. Passing the law office, they got a wave from Eagle Junction's new marshal, Cyrus Hanley.

'Where are we headed, Dan?' Mary asked.

'Might as well call me Josh,' he said. 'Most everyone is.'

'If you folks need another name,' Emily smiled. 'How about Clancy?'

After a long silence Dan said, 'Where are we headed, huh?' He hugged Mary and Emily to him. 'A place called happiness, I guess.'

Mary kissed him on the right cheek – Emily on the left, and Josh Lawson knew that he had already arrived at that place called happiness, made all the sweeter by the bulge of Flint's Bounty in his pocket.